Death in the Devil's Range

Michael L. Patton

All rights reserved.
ISBN-10: 1979144397
ISBN-13: 978-1979144391

DEDICATION

This book is dedicated to my wife Audrey and my sister Annette. The two kindest and strongest women in my life.

CONTENTS

Contents

ACKNOWLEDGMENTS

I have had help from a number of people in delving into my first novel. I would like to acknowledge the East Bay Writer's Group, which has helped and educated me tremendously. Special thanks to Mel Stolhand and John Taylor for taking me under their wings. Thanks to my many friends for their reviews of the early, painful drafts. Special thanks to Don and Gary Harmon for their antics and inspiration

CHAPTER 1 - MONDAY, MAY 10TH

Dr. Norbert Willis sat at his desk seething in frustration. He slammed the three-ring binder closed, picked up his hardbound notebook, and began furiously writing notes before the thoughts left his head. Time was running out. He knew it. Pushing eighty-eight, he could feel his body failing. He reached up and touched the Band-Aid on his forehead as a physical reminder of his most recent misadventure— sliding his Jeep off an easy trail and bending the fender on a boulder.

Thinking back over his career, he enjoyed plenty of success, starting as a young physicist just as World War II was ending. He was the youngest graduate in his class and went on to a brilliant career, ending up at Lawrence Livermore National Laboratory. Often bristling at the restrictions the government bureaucrats imposed on his work until he retired almost twenty years ago, he was now combing through documents he had snuck out of the labs since then. They had nothing to do with physics. His work in the late 1940s and 1950s in physics gave him access to many of the Nazi documents in an attempt to learn their secrets and track down their scientists. One of his assignments was trying to reconstruct the movements of scientific personnel and equipment in the last hectic days of the war. He stopped writing and looked around at the private study he built with his own hands. It started out in the 1950s as a bomb shelter, but served him well as a safe place to hide the documents that were not supposed to be in his possession, and provided him a private place to work.

During his work on the shipments, he learned that Nazi submarines were used to transport uranium to Japan. The records showed that the Japanese paid in gold bullion that was brought back using the same subs. A few of them were lost near Argentina. It soon became his retirement hobby to try to find the lost subs and the bullion that would be worth billions now. Even if he turned it over, his share for locating it would make him a wealthy man. He made a few trips to South America to search for any clues or eyewitnesses.

He felt for years that he was close to uncovering this great secret. He would not let it beat him. Willis glanced up at the map above his desk. The colored pushpins encoded specific locations known only to him. He swore to himself and began scribbling frantically in his lab book. This continued until exhausted, the old man hobbled over to the recliner that had been rescued before his wife could throw it out. He sat and reviewed his notes, then entered one last thought before shutting the book. Little did he know it would be his final entry. He needed a minute to rest his eyes, to think, but instead fell asleep. The lab book slid from his hand, down beside the seat of the recliner and wedged between the cushion and the arm.

He awoke with a start. Looking around, he was calmed by the familiar surroundings of his books and his research. A memory popped into his head causing him to hurriedly move to the desk to capture it before it was gone. Where the hell was his notebook? He always left it right here. He glanced back at the recliner, but it was deep between the cushions now and not visible from his desk. Damn old age, anyway.

~ ~ ~ ~

"I'm telling you, this is the smartest dog in the world." Dan Williams looked at his uncle with a twinkle in his eye.

His Uncle Wally had driven from Modesto to meet Dan at his house and help him haul some things to Dan's machine shop. Wally was his father's brother, and Dan grew up helping them work on cars and other projects in Modesto. Dan now lived on a ranch in the hills east of San Jose owned by his mom's brother. The shop was on the primary portion of the spread, located about an hour southeast of Oakland.

"I call bullshit." Uncle Wally shook his head in disbelief. "What can she do that is so brilliant?"

Dan unclipped his cell phone from the plastic holster on his belt and handed it to his skeptical uncle. "You take this and put it in the other room. You can even put it under something and she'll find it."

"Yeah, right," Uncle Wally said, sarcasm dripping from his words as he reluctantly took the phone. He disappeared into the bedroom around the corner.

Syd was a female cattle dog, a mix of Australian Shepherd and mutt, with one ear that stood up and one that flopped lazily on her forehead. She had pale blue eyes that watched closely as Wally exited the room. She played this game with Dan often, so she was anxiously awaiting the command to retrieve.

"Make it fair. Don't go burying it under the mattress or something," Dan called after him.

A few minutes later, Wally came out of the bedroom smirking. "Okay, hotshot, let's see Syd the Wonderdog find that phone now."

Dan looked over at the dog, who was staring intently at her owner waiting for the signal. "Syd, go get my phone, girl." Syd was around the corner before he finished speaking the command. Within a few seconds, she proudly pranced back into the room and dropped the cell phone on Dan's lap. "Good girl." Dan scratched her ears as he praised the dog.

"I'll be a son of a…" Wally looked at the phone in disbelief. "Did you rub dog food on that thing or something?"

"No, but maybe she does smell me on it, or the scent of the plastic. Who knows?"

3

"I kinda doubt that." Wally smiled at Dan. "I stuck it down in one of your boots in the front of the closet. The boot would smell more like you than the phone." He rubbed his chin. "Tell you what, let's try something." He walked into the other room, leaving Dan holding his phone. When he returned, he looked at Syd.

"Syd, go get my cell phone."

Syd was off in a shot and back just as quick, dropping the phone at Uncle Wally's feet.

"That dog's pretty smart. I'll give you that." He looked at Dan. "I laid it on the bed, but I still think she's going by smell."

"Could be." Dan scratched Syd's ears. "I'd never tried it with someone else's phone. I trained her because I'm always leaving mine in the next room, or in my truck. She can find my keys too. Watch." Dan stood up and felt his pockets like he was searching for something. Syd immediately perked up again.

"What am I missing, Syd?" He continued to pat his pockets. "My keys and my wallet. Get 'em, girl." Syd stood up and scoured the room, then went into Dan's bedroom. She returned with both, the keyring draped around one of her lower canine teeth, and the wallet grasped in her jaw. Dan smiled at Wally and said nothing.

"Well she's smarter than her owner, I'll give her that." Uncle Wally smiled. "Now, you ready to get some work done?"

"C'mon, Syd. Mount up." Dan opened the door and Syd shot out and leaped up into the bed of Dan's pickup parked in the driveway.

~ ~ ~ ~

No one seemed to pay him much attention on the plane, but Albert Stevens was a quirky little man. Barely breaking five foot two, his stature belied his goals in life and his sense of purpose. Meticulous in his dress, his shirts were always white and his pants creased to a laser-sharp line. Wire-rimmed glasses only seemed to intensify the blueness of his eyes, which were continually moving to take in his surroundings. He wore his shirts loose masking his muscular physique. When he occasionally rolled up his shirtsleeves, his forearms revealed he was a man who could drive a nail with one blow of a hammer. He walked a bit like a rooster, his chest leading the way. He was determined and efficient in his movements and his words. Taking his seat on the plane, he quickly reviewed his files, put them away and listened to the classical music channel the airline provided.

His mission was clear. He needed to find out what information the old man has and to prevent by any means the continuation of any leaks. He dedicated himself to stopping anyone from learning the organization's secrets. These misguided people were more dangerous than they knew. If he found anything, he would call in a team to address the situation. Albert liked being the point man and took his job very seriously.

They landed at Oakland International Airport, and since he only brought a carry-on proceeded directly to the National bus. His frequent travels made him an Emerald Club member. However, the real value of this membership was he could pick discrete vehicles that would not stand out. He walked up to a white four-door, mid-sized sedan and threw his carry-on bag in the back seat. No need to stand out. He was your average businessman on a Monday morning flight to the West Coast. In contrast, the guy behind him at the exit booth of the National parking lot was driving a new yellow Camaro convertible. People would notice and remember such a car, but that's probably why the young hot dog in the car wanted it. Albert showed his papers to the employee at the booth and pulled away chuckling.

~ ~ ~ ~

Paulo was not thrilled with the rental car choice, but rarely having traveled to the US, he had no status with the local companies. He asked for a gray sedan but was told the yellow Camaro was all they had. Any other time Paulo would love to have the new Camaro convertible but not today. Now, he would need to use more aggressive techniques to accomplish his task.

He kept an eye on the white sedan as it left the booth and watched it make a right turn at the second light. He was lucky the counter was not busy when he arrived or he would have already lost his prey. He could not let the clueless little man get away from him. Paulo needed to get the information before he did.

He breezed through the booth since he received his paperwork at the counter. He made the second right, and as luck would have it, the white sedan pulled into a gas station about a quarter mile ahead. Time to activate plan B.

Paulo entered the gas station lot and watched Albert walk straight into the convenience store it included. The rental car would obviously not need fuel yet. Paulo got out of the car and acted as if he was getting something from the trunk, then bent down to tie his shoe between the sedans. The glass front of the convenience store looked out onto the parking lot and the pumps. Americans. They never missed a chance to try to sell you something. He could see his subject inside heading to the tall, glass coolers along the far wall. The cars blocked the view from the store, so he discreetly bent down and put a tracking device on the rear wheel well of the sedan. Perhaps his luck was going to hold out this trip. He walked inside, moving just past his target, almost touching him, and went to the bottled water. Flying always dehydrated him.

The clerk behind the counter was a young Hispanic girl, most likely of Mexican descent. She seemed a little shocked when he, a tall man with blondish, thinning hair, spoke to her in English with a Hispanic accent.   He returned to the Camaro and activated the software on his laptop that would track the device he planted. He was getting a clear signal, which would help neutralize the flashy ride as he could follow from a distance now. Driving along he noticed there were quite a few Camaros in the area, though not many convertibles. Maybe he would be able to blend in.

Paulo would not let his country, his family and, most importantly, his grandfather down. His immediate goal was to follow this quirky little man whose name he knew was Stevens. Paulo hoped he could tail Stevens to that nosy scientist. Finding the scientist could hold the key to the ultimate success of the mission. He would find this arrogant American scientist who was part of the organization that had already taken so much from his family, who had dared come to his country to hunt for treasure that was his birthright, and he would snatch the prize right from under him.

CHAPTER 2 - MONDAY MIDMORNING

Dan pulled off the road and across the cattle guard onto the main ranch. The house was off to the left as he descended the hill and the rumble of his pickup caused his aunt to look up as she puttered in the yard. Both waved, but Dan turned right at the bottom of the drive and headed to the shop. Syd barked a greeting to the ranch dogs as they scrambled to chase the truck. Typically, Dan would head over to chat, but he had a busy schedule today. He was only weeks away from a project deadline and was running behind because of problems getting some materials in time.

He thought about how much he enjoyed the freedom ranch work gave him to determine his schedule. The ranch was his Uncle Ed's. Dan was brought into his uncle's ranching business ten years ago, when he and his wife, Janet, just married. Never one to shy away from work, Dan soon became indispensable. He was a whiz when it came to fixing things and easily kept up his end of the chores. In return, the hard work gradually built up his shoulders and arms converting him from a tall skinny youngster to a man with broad shoulders, able to throw 120-pound hay bales around all afternoon. They became so close his uncle requested Dan refer to him as Ed instead of Uncle. After Janet had been killed in a car accident five years ago, Ed's support kept him going through the hard times.

Ed bought the ranch in the mid-1950s, starting with 40 acres and parlaying that over the years into over 13,000 acres. It consisted of a significant portion of the southern San Antonio Valley, and an eastern section named the Hawk's Nest for its views that wrapped down on the Patterson side of the hills. Called the Rockin' A Ranch, the previous owner, whose family settled it in the late 1890s, had a wife named Audrey and a sister named Annie. Annie lived on the

Rockin' A in a separate house, but they always ate meals together. The previous owner told Ed his favorite time of the day was when he came home to find both of them sitting on the front porch in their rocking chairs. They were usually stringing green beans or some other chore to keep their hands busy. He named the Rockin' A after the two most important women in his life. Ed thought it was a great story, so he kept the name. To this day the locals referred to him as the new owner of the Rockin' A.

Two years ago Dan started collecting machining tools to help make some parts they needed for equipment. As the collection grew, he worked with Ed to create a space in a large storage building to set up a small shop. He first bought a lathe, then a milling machine. Eventually, it grew so big they built a large Quonset hut divided into a metal shop, a woodworking area and a vehicle repair area complete with a car lift.

As Dan's skills improved, and with the equipment they installed, soon everyone in the area was stopping by with problems and projects for him. What began as tinkering on weekends and evenings developed into a small business, though Dan often didn't charge the local folks. He and Ed jokingly called it HillTek Incorporated because of being up in the hills. As word spread it eventually became almost a full-time job doing machine work, so Dan pulled in Wally to help out when needed.

He took a detour on route to the main ranch so he could look in on some calves Ed asked him to check. He smiled to see his Uncle Wally already beat him to the shop. He knew he would take some grief for taking longer to get there. Wally was quite the character, always with a story or joke to tell, and they developed a close rapport that allowed them to get a lot of work done and have a good time doing it. Dan was around Wally much more as he entered his thirties and they had gotten much closer. He referred to him as Uncle, or sometimes as Papi, which he copied from Wally's granddaughter.

"You doing okay, Uncle?" Dan asked as entered the door of the shop.

"I feel more like I do right now than I did a while ago," Wally quipped.

Dan gave an eye roll as he continued into the shop. Papi had a million sayings primarily designed to see if you were listening, or get a reaction. Best not to encourage him this early in the morning, Dan thought as he put on his work apron. "What have you screwed up so far?"

"Oh, I just got here a few minutes ago, but I was gonna start measuring and marking those pieces for that roll cage. Are you late because you stopped at the powder coater?"

"First of all, I'm not late, because I'm the boss. And second, I asked you to stop and pick up the powder coating," Dan said in mock anger. Dan would have to rethink what he planned to do today because he needed the powder-coated parts to start assembly of the project coming due. Syd ignored them, going to a shaded corner of the shop and lying down.

"You mean to tell me that a young man like yourself can't beat an old man like me to work because you were too busy blow-drying your hair?" Wally said, smiling. He changed his tone because he saw the look on Dan's face. "I picked the powder coating up yesterday. It's in the bed of my truck."

Having established the tone for the day, both men set about their work with smiles on their faces.

~ ~ ~ ~

Albert was grateful for the navigation system in the rental car. After taking several interstates from the airport, he headed out into the suburbs. Albert would not have found the road leading south out of the town of Livermore into the hills without it. Though labeled Mines Road, he could see no evidence of mines. Perhaps they were farther along. As the road climbed, it became apparent a change of vehicles would be needed. This far out in the country the new car would stand out. Albert grew up in a similar area on the East Coast, a rural part of West Virginia. People in these areas knew each other and would notice outsiders roaming around. He would have to come up with something to fit in easier. Most people up here drove pickup trucks out of necessity, as they were primarily ranchers.

He continued, venturing close to thirty miles on Mines Road before coming to another road going off to the left. Just before the intersection was a small building with neon beer signs in the window. The sign out front proclaimed it as Sam's Place. It was the first sign of civilization Albert had seen other than a few houses, and he began to wonder if he was getting lost. His navigation system said he had about ten miles to go, but it recalculated several times in the hills when he must have lost line of sight with the satellites.

He was tempted to stop but drove on to get the lay of the land. He noticed the area flattened out into a beautiful little valley after passing Sam's Place. As the valley spread before him, there were a few more houses. Eventually, the address numbers on the mailboxes were getting close to the address he was seeking. His confidence climbed when a few miles up the road a mailbox appeared on the left-hand side with the correct number and the name Willis written on it.

I guess Willis is old-school enough he's not as concerned with security as most town people are nowadays. Personally, Albert loved country living. He drove past to see if he could gain a better view of his target. The road did not oblige him, so Albert turned around and pulled to the shoulder to get a feel for the place. Since it was midafternoon, he was afraid to leave his car and walk in because someone could spot him. There was no phone coverage to use Google to find how far the house would be down the dirt access road. He could check it at the hotel and come back early tomorrow before daylight.

~ ~ ~ ~

Paulo cautiously followed the white sedan, leaving almost half a mile between them, cursing his flashy rental car. Fortunately, the signal was still strong and Stevens used only interstates once he left the airport. That changed, however, once off the interstate at Livermore when the target started heading south. Paulo followed him until he turned onto a small country road into the hills. As soon as the signal made a right onto Mines Road, Paulo pulled off to the side. There was no way he could stay incognito in this car. If the white car turned around or backtracked, he would likely be made.

Paulo was nothing if not decisive. He turned around and headed toward downtown, having noticed a few wineries nearby. Pulling the Camaro into one of the tasting room parking lots, Paulo walked toward some nearby grape vines, acting interested in them. With a soft briefcase containing a laptop in hand, he tried to look like a salesman visiting the winery to close a deal.

Ducking around the corner of the tasting room, he walked toward the production facilities of the winery. Since it was May there were very few people working in the production area. There, ahead, sat the gray trucks he spied from the road. The pickups were lined up near a loading dock for the staff to run errands. Paulo slid into the first one and checked the ignition. No keys. He pulled the visor down and the keys dropped into his lap. God bless trusting Americans.

He left the facility and headed in the direction Stevens went. Paulo figured that his car would be safe in the parking lot with all the other wine tasters at least until they closed. The laptop did not pick up the signal again for a few miles, and even then it was weak and intermittent. It wasn't until he came to a group of houses and what looked like a small bar that the signal became stronger. He liked this little valley out in the middle of nowhere. Continuing a few miles the signal strength increased even more. He passed the white sedan sitting beside the road, heading in the opposite direction. Congratulating himself for switching vehicles, he put on a baseball cap with the winery's logo on it he found on the dashboard of the truck. He was sure the changes would keep him from being noticed.

He spotted the name on a large gray mailbox that was ten yards past the sedan. Willis. He recognized it as the name of the scientist his grandfather had mentioned. Willis was the man he was really trying to find and following Stevens had paid off. Paulo continued on until he was out of sight, watching the monitor to ensure the small blip on the screen didn't move. It didn't, so he was confident he was viewed as another local.

When the sedan finally did move, it went south at a casual pace and stopped at the little bar/restaurant called Sam's Place. Following, Paulo drove past the bar and pulled off on a dirt track until he was hidden from the road. He waited there to see what Stevens did next since it was still early afternoon and to ensure that Stevens did not try to contact Willis before Paulo could get to him. He planned to make his approach early the next morning when there was no one around.

~ ~ ~ ~

Albert pulled into the parking lot of Sam's Place and parked near a large oak tree at the right edge of the property. The only other cars in the lot were an older model, brown pickup and an all-wheel-drive Subaru station wagon. It was midafternoon, likely not the busiest time for the place. The building, once a house, had been converted into a restaurant of sorts. There were picnic tables off to the left as he walked up to the steps. He couldn't imagine a place so far out in the country would have overflow crowds that would require outside seating. Perhaps it was used during warm weather. There were even horseshoe pits, though he could see no horseshoes in them.

The bar looked just as rustic inside. It took a few seconds for his eyes to adjust to the room after being out in the bright sunlight. It was not shabby, but definitely rural with wild boars' heads mounted on the wall and a framed display of arrowheads. A couple of ceiling fans spun lazily overhead. A woman in her thirties with brown hair casually greeted him. She informed him that she was Sam, or Samantha, the owner and that she'd bought the place from a local family who ran it since the 1960s. Sam wore minimal makeup, with a girl-next-door cuteness about her. She gave him a menu and instructed him to sit anywhere he wished.

After ordering a burger and a Coke, he sat at the far end of the bar and pretended to be absorbed in a sports channel playing on the television. At the other end of the bar were what appeared to be a couple of locals. Both wore jeans and boots, though one guy wore a ball cap with CAT on the front and looked like he was wrestling something in the mud earlier. The other was taller and wore a cowboy hat with the ease and set of someone who did most of his work from a horse. His voice was slightly high-pitched, with enough of a twang that he sounded like the real deal. Any other time, Albert would have loved to talk with him to get more of a local flavor, but he did not want to attract too much attention so he made no effort to engage.

"What's this I hear about the USGS poking around out here again?" the tall cowboy said to the other. "Burt said he was at a meeting in town and they were comin' up here to measure somethin'."

"No idea," the other replied. "It's probably some excuse for the damned government to look for pot growers."

"Aw, hell. The cops use helicopters to do that."

"Well, I don't know. Could be anything."

Albert didn't react, but the overheard exchange gave him an idea. Finishing his lunch, he paid his bill. As he was getting up to walk out, a man came through the door. The man was almost as tall as the cowboy but looked more muscular through the shoulders. His jeans were relatively clean and he wore a Western-style shirt with buttons instead of the usual snaps. His quick smile acknowledged the two guys at the bar. The woman behind the counter brightened considerably.

"Hey, Dan. What can I get ya?" she offered.

"Nothing for me, Sam, thanks." He seemed not to notice her interest. "I was just checking to see if those parts I ordered were delivered by UPS today."

"UPS hasn't come yet. Should be showin' up anytime."

"Okay, maybe I will have a Dr. Pepper while I wait for a bit." He nodded as Albert passed him.

Sam brought him a Dr. Pepper and a balled-up napkin. When he looked at it funny, she said, "It's some chicken for Syd." He smiled, shook his head and put it in his shirt pocket.

~ ~ ~ ~

Paulo was glad he grabbed some trail mix and an energy bar at the gas station with his water. He ate them as he waited for the sedan to move again. When it passed his hiding place on a dirt road, Paulo stayed until there would be a safe cushion between the two vehicles. He maintained the distance for the thirty miles of winding road returning to Livermore. At the end of Mines Road, Paulo pulled into the winery, left the truck in the visitors' parking lot and casually walked over to the yellow Camaro, carrying his briefcase with his laptop inside. Pulling out of the winery, he noticed on his screen that Stevens was stopped near the interstate a few miles ahead. When he got close to the area, he could see the sedan pulled into a cluster of hotels and chain restaurants. Paulo selected a hotel across the side street and requested a room overlooking the parking lot.

Intent on ditching the flashy car, he called the rental agency and told them he had a flat tire and asked them to send a replacement when they could. They were happy to inform him they had a satellite franchise in the town of Livermore, where he was located, and could be there in fifteen minutes with a different car. Paulo hurried down to the car and let the air out of the left front tire. A short time later, an eager young man from the agency pulled up in a small, tan Jeep Compass. They switched keys and Paulo signed the paperwork. He left the youngster to struggle with putting the mini-spare on the Camaro. The kid looked excited to get his hands on the bright yellow sports car. One problem solved.

Paulo took the SUV, got some fast food for dinner and went to his hotel room to keep an eye on Stevens. Tired from the flight, he was glad to see the target walk across the street to a chain restaurant. He set his alarm for 4:30 a.m. and lay down on the bed. The software on the laptop would alert him if the sedan started moving again.

Sure enough, the laptop screeched about an hour later. Paulo jumped up from the bed and looked out the window in time to see the sedan pull out of the parking lot. He was still half asleep so was initially confused when he saw Stevens standing in the parking lot. *What was he doing?* Paulo shook his head trying to clarify his thinking.

Stevens was standing next to a white SUV similar to the one Paulo had just received. This new vehicle was also a Jeep, but a different model and a little bigger. The insignia said Cherokee. Stevens measured an area on the driver's door with a tape measure. *So I was*

17

not the only one to decide to switch vehicles. Looking through his binoculars, he watched as his target set a laptop on the hood of the new car and worked on what looked like graphic design. Once happy with his work, Stevens walked across the street to a FedEx Office store. A short while later he returned to the Cherokee and placed a small sign in the area he previously measured. Standing back, Stevens inspected his work. He would now be driving an SUV with a USGS logo on the side.

Paulo waited until Stevens left and was inside for thirty minutes before taking the chance to go near the new vehicle. Glad he brought two additional tracking devices in case of problems, he placed the magnetic device on the undercarriage of the Cherokee and went to his room. The signal was as strong as the first one. He set it to alarm when moved and returned to bed.☐

CHAPTER 3 - TUESDAY, MAY 11TH

Dan and Wally both looked up from their work as Ed's truck came sliding to a stop in front of the shop, a cloud of dust billowing in from the dry heat. It was only 9:30 a.m., but the morning coolness had already burned off. It was going to be a warm one.

"What the hell?" Dan said as he shut off the lathe. Syd stood up, looking at the truck as it rocked to a stop.

"That ain't like him," Wally observed. "Somethin's up." Wally set down the tape measure he was using to mark the next batch of steel he planned to cut. They both moved toward the open overhead door. Ed jumped out of his truck as it still rocked from being put into park so abruptly. In his mid-seventies, ranch life kept Ed in shape, making most people think he was ten to fifteen years younger. A gregarious man, who loved to tell stories of his days as a hot-rodder or the many hunting trips he'd experienced, he was not easily excited, which drew attention to his behavior now.

"Dan, grab the high-lift jack off your truck and get in. Betty called and said a car fell on Willis." He grabbed a pry bar and a bottle jack out of the shop and headed toward the door.

"You want me to go too?" Wally asked, knowing it was something serious by Ed's demeanor.

"Sure. Jump in, but we have to hurry."

Dan was already throwing the hi-lift jack from his 4x4 onto the bed of Ed's truck and climbed into the passenger seat as Wally scrambled into the back seat of the one-ton Chevy crew cab. Syd hopped onto the flatbed with Ed's dog, Rounder. Dan knew better than to ask a bunch of questions when Ed was this intense. He would give them details when he was ready. Ed backed the truck away from the shop entrance and slammed it into gear, fishtailing in the gravel driveway as they shot onto the pavement. Once on the solid road and progressing at a steady speed, Ed finally broke the silence.

"She just called. She was hysterical and not making much sense. I told her we were on the way."

"Did she call for an ambulance?" Wally asked from the back seat.

"Said she called me first. I told her to call 911 and we'd be there as fast as we could."

Willis and Betty lived about four miles away, but it could take the sheriff thirty minutes or more to get to the area. While only about fifteen miles from San Jose as the crow flies, the San Antonio Valley was a world away from the high-tech Silicon Valley. Nestled in the Diablo Range, there is only one twisty road in and out of the area, which kept it sparsely populated with cattle ranchers and independent-minded individuals who prefer solitude to people.

"I wonder if something happened with his Jeep again," Dan said. A look from Ed caused him to continue. "He stopped in the shop yesterday. Borrowed a couple of tools. He said he slid on a hill over by the Castle Rock last Friday and dinged his fender on a boulder."

"I told him to stop taking that thing over there, that's rough country for a man his age," Ed grumbled.

He turned off onto the dirt track leading to Willis's property, dust flying up behind them. As they approached the house a few minutes later, they could see Betty out by the separate garage/shop off to the left. Betty waved them over to the open garage door. As soon as they got in the door, Ed stopped in his tracks. Looking over Ed's shoulder, Dan's heart dropped. What they saw was far more gruesome than expected.

CHAPTER 4 - TUESDAY MIDMORNING

Norbert Willis lay on the floor of his garage. His head was crushed by the rail of a four-post car lift with an older Jeep CJ on it. A pool of blood spread from under the body.

Betty was hysterical, shouting, "You've got to help! Help him!"

Ed stepped forward. He bent down and felt for a pulse in Willis's wrist, stood and turned to Betty. "Betty, I'm sorry. We're too late. He's been gone awhile because he's cold. There's nothing we can do."

"Well at least get this damned thing off him." She burst into tears and Ed grabbed her by the arms as her knees began to buckle. He turned her and began to move her toward the door. Dan caught his eye as they walked past. A slight shake of Ed's head was enough to tell Dan not to bother.

"Everybody clear out of here 'til the sheriff arrives." Ed herded them out the door. They could do nothing now except wait for the authorities.

The California Department of Forestry, or CDF, fire crew arrived a few minutes later with their EMT and Dan informed them they were too late to do anything. The EMT went in to confirm the lack of pulse, then shook his head. Dan and Wally followed him in to act as witnesses, ensuring nothing else was disturbed. Silent, they walked out to join the others. Ed took Betty in the house and attempted to comfort her. He was at a loss for what to say to a woman wavering between hysterics and anger, so he called his wife Margaret to come over. Maybe she could keep Betty calm until some family arrived.

The CDF crew waited for the sheriff to give their report. "How'd you guys get here so fast?" one of them asked no one in particular.

"Betty called Ed first," answered Dan.

"Why would anyone call him before calling 911?" he questioned, perplexed.

"Maybe because she knew she would get someone on the other end of the phone who gives a damn," Wally said, not liking the implication. "Do you see how long it takes the sheriff to get here?"

Dan grabbed Wally by the arm to calm him down. The CDF guy put his hands up in surrender and walked to his group. An uneasy silence descended until Dan went over to the CDF crew.

"Sorry, guys, my uncle's obviously upset. We appreciate you guys being here and the service you provide to the folks up here." They seemed to relax a bit, but the one who raised the question kept a wary eye on Wally.

Margaret pulled in and went directly into the house, allowing Ed to slip out a few minutes later. Finally, a sheriff's vehicle pulled in, dust billowing around the marked Ford SUV, lights flashing. A sheriff's Crown Victoria followed the SUV and came sliding to a dramatic stop behind the first vehicle. Out of the second car popped a short deputy rushing to put his hat on. He practically tripped over his nightstick when he missed its baton ring on his belt.

"Oh jeez," said Dan, shaking his head. "Here comes Barney Fife."

Deputy Spinelli was five foot six and stocky with close-cropped black hair and a short mustache. He was known locally as Speedy, both because he tended to speak rapidly and for his propensity to give out speeding tickets at marginal speeds above the limit. Spinelli looked nothing like the deputy from the 1960s TV show but had a similar reputation for overreacting. He fell in behind Lieutenant Thronson as they strode toward the group outside the garage. Thronson was a big man, his blond hair and blue eyes signifying his Swedish descent. His easy-going manner made him tolerable to the folks in the hills. He walked up and shook hands with Ed, then the CDF EMT. He turned and nodded to the others.

"What've we got?" he asked, waiting for one of the other two to start talking. Ed gave him the rundown of being called and what they found when they got there. Ed also made sure to tell him that other than feeling for a pulse they touched nothing and came outside to wait.

"Dead huh?" Thronson shook his head. He was not looking forward to going into the garage. Spinelli, on the other hand, started twitching like a terrier that saw a squirrel, putting his hand on his gun and staring at the garage door waiting for Thronson to move. Thronson listened as the EMT gave his report then dismissed the CDF crew to go about their business. As they walked to their truck, Thronson nodded at Ed, Dan, and Wally. "OK, you three come with me."

Walking through the door, Thronson pointed to his left. "You three stand over there out of the way." He and Spinelli went over to examine the body, not speaking at all. After looking around, squatting down to get a closer look and circling the whole shop, Spinelli moved toward the three of them.

"Looks to me like we can't rule out suicide," he announced, seemingly talking to Thronson but toward the group for effect. "But—"

Before he could get out anything else, Wally launched into a tirade. "How many kinds of stupid are you?" He paused. Behind Spinelli, Thronson smirked but said nothing. "So you think the man killed himself by sticking his head under the rail and crushing it here," he said, pointing for clarification. "While the switch to activate it is over there ten feet away." He pointed to the other side of the lift. He paused to let it sink in. "Personally, I don't think his arms are long enough, and at almost ninety years old I don't think he'd be fast enough to get under it before it stopped moving."

Spinelli looked incredulous, having no idea how the lift worked. "Perhaps it malfunctioned. We'll have to test it."

"You just do that." Wally was not backing down.

Thronson interrupted by saying, "We will need to check the system for any defects or malfunctions that could have caused this. But let's not rule it out until we get more information. Before we proceed, I need the lab guys to work over the whole scene. What I need from you three is to tell me exactly how far into this room you came this morning. Did you touch anything? Move anything?"

The three of them explained that Dan and Wally were no farther in than they currently were and only Ed had touched the body.

"Have you been in this garage before, recently?"

All three shook their heads. Suddenly, Dan remembered. "I was here about three weeks ago and helped him rebuild a carburetor for this Jeep but not since then."

"Okay, you go outside and we'll wait for the techs."

The three of them turned to file out, as Spinelli came over holding a body hammer. It had a flat face on one end for pounding surfaces, and the opposite end was a curved wedge shape. They all stopped to see what was happening.

"Lieutenant." He extended the hand with the hammer and nodded toward it. "I found this in a trash barrel. It has blood on it."

Thronson was apoplectic. "You moron. What part of 'wait for the crime techs' did you not understand? You just contaminated the scene."

"But I—"

"Shut the hell up. Get an evidence bag, put that hammer in it, give the damned thing to me then go sit in your vehicle until I come get you." He pointed to Spinelli's cruiser.

Wally shook his head. He saw Ed roll his eyes, but when Wally looked over at Dan, his nephew was as white as a ghost.

Dan watched as Spinelli went to the trunk of his cruiser and pulled out an evidence kit. He took out a plastic zip-lock bag and put the hammer in it, wrote something on the bag with a sharpie and sealed it. Having accomplished his assigned task, Spinelli walked

24

around to the front of his car, lay the bag containing the hammer on the front fender and leaned against the cruiser with his arms crossed. He looked like a scolded schoolboy who was rebelling by refusing Thronson's order to sit in his car.

There was a slight commotion behind Spinelli as a beat-up brown pickup carrying two passengers pulled into the yard. It didn't take long for word to spread in the hills and folks were showing up to see what was going on. It was Harvey and Albert, two locals, both retired with nothing better to do. Harvey was a beanpole of a man who always wore a tattered straw cowboy hat and tended to stutter. His friend Albert was short, overweight and talked at a high-pitched rapid pace. Dan always wondered how they ever managed to become friends.

"I heard the call on my scanner," Harvey announced. "Came to see if we could help."

Deputy Spinelli spun around and went into control mode, holding up his hands to stop them. "Sorry, fellas, this is a crime scene. You can't go in there."

"Is Willis alright?" Albert asked.

"Again, this is an active investigation. We can't tell you anything."

Harvey noticed the bag on Spinelli's fender, creased his brow and blurted, "Hey, Dan, why's your hammer got blood on it?" He kept looking back and forth from the bloody tool to Dan. The hammer had the initials DW on the butt of the handle.

Ed muttered, "Oh, for Christ's sake." He looked at Wally, trying to warn him with his eyes not to say anything. But it was out of the bag.

Spinelli looked at Dan and stiffened, hand automatically going to his gun. "Is that yours?"

Dan looked at the deputy, dropped his chin and shook his head in disbelief. Behind him, Ed said, "Let's wait for the lieutenant."

Thronson had gone into the garage and was taking a few pictures with his cell phone.

Undaunted, Spinelli began moving toward Dan, right hand still on his gun strap, his left taking out his cuffs. "I guess you'll have to answer me at the station."

Dan heard Syd growl from the truck behind him. "Syd, sit." The dog settled down but kept her head up, eyes glued on Spinelli.

Ed stepped in front of Dan. "I said, let's wait for the lieutenant."

At that, Spinelli stopped in his tracks but unsnapped the strap holding his weapon. Ed looked him in the eye and with a calm voice said, "Son, around here, if you pull a gun on a man, you'd better be ready to use it." He paused but stood his ground. "Now, here's what's gonna happen. Dan is not going anywhere, and you are going to step back while I stick my head in the door and get the lieutenant. Dan will explain all about the hammer and we'll let Thronson decide who's talking to who and where." Ed was an imposing figure, at least a head taller than Spinelli.

Spinelli inched forward.

Still as calmly as if he were talking to a child, Ed continued. "Deputy, if you pull that gun, I have about four witnesses who are gonna swear the reason they found it up your ass is that you threw it on the ground and sat on it. Are we clear?"

Spinelli blinked, swallowed hard and almost squeaked, "Crystal." He took three steps backward and tried to look casual as he leaned against the fender of his cruiser again. "Lieutenant." his voice cracked.

"Yeah," Thronson answered as he came out the door. He stopped short and frowned as he looked at the postures of Spinelli, Ed, and Dan. "What's up?"

"We have a sort of development here." Spinelli was almost in control of his voice again. "This man here identified the weapon as belonging to Dan."

Thronson asked Dan, "Is that yours?"

"Yes, sir, that's my hammer. Willis stopped by yesterday, told me he'd slid his Jeep into a rock and borrowed a few tools including the hammer."

"What time was this?"

"About two yesterday afternoon. That Jeep's old, but you can see on the right rear fender where there are some new scratches. Willis wasn't the most capable four-wheeler."

"I'll check it out." He thought for a moment. "What else did he borrow?"

"A couple of dollies and a short blue pry bar. Body dollies," Dan clarified.

"Gotcha." Thronson looked around. "So what's everybody looking so twitchy about?"

Wally spoke up. "Speedy here whipped out his cuffs and was about to take Dan in, is what."

Thronson smiled at the nickname that he'd heard before. "You'll have to excuse Deputy Spinelli's enthusiasm, gentlemen. He's spent too much time in San Jose. It will take him a little while to adjust to the folks up here. So to clear this up, let's cut right to the chase." He looked directly at Dan. "Can you explain this?"

"Yes, sir." He held Thronson's gaze steadily.

"Okay, let's do that." He looked at Spinelli. "I suggest you get in your car and start on the mountain of paperwork you caused."

Spinelli reached for the hammer.

"No. Leave it there so it can't get you in any more trouble."

Spinelli said nothing but shot a look at both Wally and Dan. He made no eye contact with Ed, climbed into his car, grabbed a clipboard and acted as if he was reading the computer screen on the dash.

Syd, sensing the danger had passed, lay her head down and groaned a dog harrumph.

Thronson turned to Dan, Ed, and Wally. "You three come with

me. I want to talk to you separately, so Ed, if you don't mind waiting in your truck," he said as he nodded at Ed's truck. "Wally, you wait here by yourself." He put his hand on Dan's shoulder. "Step into my office," he said, pointing at his SUV. Thronson walked around to the driver's side. They each climbed in. Dan sat in the front passenger seat staring straight ahead.

"You mind answering a few more questions here?"

"No. Not at all." Dan shot a glance at Ed in his truck, who nodded to reassure him. Thronson advised Dan of his rights, assuring him it was merely routine procedure. It still made Dan nervous.

"Okay, just give me a rundown of where you've been today, for the record."

"I got up around 5:30, took a shower and met Wally over at the shop where we were until Ed came to get us."

Thronson talked to both Ed and Wally, making sure the others were kept separate from each other. After he had finished with all three, he called them all together. "Wait here, I need to check something." Thronson walked into the house. After about ten minutes, he came out, approached the group and let out a heavy sigh. He looked at each man briefly before speaking. "Mrs. Willis said her husband went out to his shop around 4 a.m. I guess he had a habit of getting up at odd hours when he couldn't sleep." He turned his attention to Dan. "Do you live alone? Can anyone corroborate where you were before six this morning when Wally arrived?"

A hurt look came over Dan's face. "Yes, sir, I live alone." He would have thought Thronson would remember he lost his wife in a car crash five years ago. He couldn't remember if it happened before Thronson's time in the hills. "Since Janet's accident…" He still couldn't bring himself to say death.

"I know about it, son. But hell, that was a long time ago. None of these women around here have roped you in yet? You didn't have some young filly spending the night?"

Dan turned a shade pinker. "No. Not at the moment."

"Well, you're not completely in the clear yet. I'm not taking you in, but I can't rule you out. So if you guys know anything that might shed some light on this…"

"Not a thing," Ed answered.

Thronson could see Wally shaking his head. "Okay, well keep your ears open. You guys have more idea what goes on up here than I do. I'll stop back in a few days, or you can call me."

This resulted in a lot of head nodding.

After heading into the house to check on Betty and Margaret, Ed, starting for his pickup, asked, "Anything else you need from us, Lieutenant?"

"Nah, not right now. Thanks for your help." He gave a wave to Dan and Wally as they turned to leave.

The mood on the ride home was sullen. Even the effusive Wally sat ruminating about what he had seen. Dan wondered who would hurt a man in his late eighties, and up here of all places. Willis had no enemies locally that he knew. Willis was retired from the Lawrence Livermore National Laboratories and had worked on some important stuff, but it was twenty years ago or more. Dan spent time with the old guy, listening to him talk about things he did in his career. At least the ones he was allowed to discuss since some of it was top secret.

Dan found it ironic that many of the people who passed through the area thought of the locals as hicks. Sure, there are few rednecks up in the hills, but most of the folks were either people like Willis who valued their privacy, or ranchers. Running a ranch required a lot of intelligence and business skills. Ed, for example, could talk to anyone on most subjects and hold his end of the conversation fine. Willis never had the patience for people he considered stupid, and he spent a lot of time with both Ed and Dan. The old man was never rude, he just wouldn't waste his time. Dan couldn't imagine him doing anything to deserve what happened.

As they pulled onto the Rockin' A Ranch, Ed looked at Dan. "I would try to avoid that deputy for a while if I was you."

"Hey, I wasn't the one who threatened to shove his gun up his ass," Dan shot back, grinning.

Wally chuckled loudly at the break in tension. "I been to two world fairs and a dogfight, and I ain't never seen anything as funny as that." Ed allowed himself a grin as he got out of the truck.

CHAPTER 5 - TUESDAY AFTERNOON

Dan tried to keep himself busy the rest of the day working with Wally in the shop, but his mind kept going back to the image of Willis lying there. He always enjoyed spending time with the older man, listening to him talk about places he had seen and the projects he was able to discuss. Willis possessed a sharp mind but was not the best with his hands and had told Dan how much he had appreciated Dan's ability to fix about anything and to work around problems that always seemed to arise. There was a mutual respect between the two men that came from working and solving problems together. He could not imagine why anyone would harm the old guy, and the fact Spinelli would implicate him added insult to injury.

When three o'clock rolled around, he told Wally, "Let's call it a day. I've got a couple of errands I need to run."

"Well, okay. What time do you want me up here tomorrow?"

Dan thought for a minute. "I need to drop some more stuff off at the powder coater tomorrow, so how about I pick you up at your place around eight?"

"That'll work. Do you need any help with your errands?"

"No, just a couple small things I need to take care of."

Wally started to head toward the door. "Oh, I need to check on my chain that's soaking." He walked over to a blue, plastic, fifty-gallon barrel cut off so that it was about fourteen inches tall, filled with an amber liquid. Wally reached down and pulled out the end of a large chain. It looked similar to a bicycle chain but was about five times the size and probably twenty feet long.

"What are you doing there?" Dan asked.

"I'm soaking this chain in kerosene to loosen it up and clean off the grease. It's from my friend Sal's car lift. It kept bunching up and

31

jerking the lift because his shop roof leaked and the chain got rusty." He inspected the chain. "Looks a lot better now," Wally said as he began wiping it with a rag and folding it into a thick cardboard box. "A little grease and it will be as good as new."

"Well, don't be leaving open barrels of kerosene lying around my shop, Papi. Get rid of it." Dan didn't care but was giving Wally a hard time. "I run a tight ship around here."

Wally busied himself with loading the restored chain in the bed of his pickup. "You give me any more crap, and I'll dump it in that Dodge's fuel tank." He gestured toward Dan's truck.

"You kidding me? That Dodge will run on goat piss. That's a man's truck." They both laughed.

"Okay, see you in the morning." Wally grabbed his ever-present ice chest of cold soft drinks and headed out to his truck. Dan closed the shop door and waved as he walked to his pickup. Syd hopped into the bed, her tongue hanging out in a happy dog smile.

Dan knew that Margaret had come back from the Willis place about one-thirty, so he stopped at the house to ask how Betty was doing. Margaret said some of the other neighbor ladies came over to keep Betty company and she was managing as best as she could. Dan wanted to help somehow but worried about going there since the dark cloud of suspicion, no matter how ill-founded, hung over him. As he left to drive over to the Hawk's Nest, he came up with an idea. He turned off at the entrance to the Willis property.

When he pulled up to the Willis house, he could see Thronson was gone, as was the yellow crime scene tape from the garage/shop. That meant the crime techs had finished. There was only one extra car in the driveway, which he recognized as belonging to the Willises' only grandson. Chucky must have come up from San Jose this morning after finding out. Dan told Syd to stay in the truck. As Dan approached the door, both Chucky and Betty came out of the house. Chucky was carrying a suitcase.

"Hey, Dan, we were just leaving. I'm taking Mom to my place for a while. I was gonna call you to see if you wouldn't mind keeping an eye on the place. My dad is flying in tonight."

"First, I want to say how sorry I am for your loss." Dan didn't know what else to say. "I guess I should talk to you about watching the place. 'Cause they found my——"

"Oh, I heard about the hammer. Speedy is an idiot, but I can see your point."

Dan smiled. "I'll make sure Ed and other neighbors keep an eye on the place, not to worry. It's just that I probably shouldn't be wandering around too much."

"Thanks, Dan." He shook Dan's hand and turned to escort Betty.

"While you're here, Chucky, can I ask you a favor along those lines?"

"Sure."

"I brought my video camera." He hesitated. "I'd like to record the inside of the garage, but I want a witness to verify I didn't disturb anything when I record it. I know it's a lot to ask, but I feel like I need to do something. I don't like how the sheriff's department is jumping to conclusions. If they already think it was me, they might not look hard enough at things. I helped your grandfather a few weeks ago with something and am familiar with the shop. I thought I might be able to help see if anything is missing. They wouldn't let me look today. If I record it so I could study it later…"

Betty spoke for the first time. "Oh, Dan, I don't think I can go back in there right now."

"Oh, no ma'am, I wouldn't ask you. I was hoping Chucky wouldn't mind witnessing. You don't have to go in. Just stand where you can see what I'm doing," he assured them. "It should only take a minute or two."

"I can do that, if it could help you catch who did this," Chucky agreed. "Grandmom, you stay here in the car."

33

With that, they settled Betty into the car and walked over to the garage, but both instinctively hesitated before entering.

"You realize they can use your recording against you, don't you?" Chucky asked.

"Yes, but since I didn't do anything, I'd feel better if I can see things myself," Dan replied. "Have you been in there? I don't want to cause any problems for you."

"I peeked in, but they chased me out when they were here. I'd like to look around to see if anything was taken, to be honest."

Dan turned on his video recorder, spoke the date and time, and stated his name and who was witnessing. Chucky stepped inside the door but hesitated when he saw the chalk outline where his grandfather had been. Dan glanced over to see if he was alright. Pain and shock were written on his face, as it became all too real.

"Just stay there. I'll do a brief walk around the shop and we'll get out of here," Dan said, putting a hand on the younger man's shoulder. His eyes fixed on the outline, Chucky nodded in response to Dan's suggestion.

Dan methodically walked around the Jeep, scanning carefully to get everything in the garage, including where the tools and parts lay. He went to Chucky and eased him out of the building. At the last minute, he also decided to walk around the outside of the building while he continued to record, with his witness following a few steps behind.

"I'm sorry that was so hard." He put his arm around Chucky's shoulder.

"I gotta face it sooner or later."

"Thanks, Chuck."

"Hey." He brightened a little. "Do you realize I am thirty-two years old and that's the first time you called me Chuck instead of Chucky?"

Dan smiled. "Well, Chuck it is from now on then."

34

They climbed into their vehicles and Dan followed them out to the road. The Willises turned left toward San Jose and Dan turned right to head home. As he was passing Sam's Place, he noticed an older blue Ford Explorer parked in the lot. He swung the truck into the parking lot and went inside. There were a few locals in the bar, the after-work crowd stopping in for a few beers. He noticed Steve and Sam talking at the far end of the bar. Steve delivered the mail, though it only ran three days a week up in the hills. He also helped out at Sam's Place on the weekends, when the motorcycle and bicycle crowds showed. In his late twenties, Steve was a good kid but liked to party more than to work. Dan, though only a few years older, had little in common with him. As he expected, they were talking about Willis.

"Hey, guys. Unbelievable, huh?" Dan sat on a nearby stool.

"Willis? Yeah, we were just talking about it," Steve answered first.

"You're normally out pretty early in the morning. Did you see anything or anyone unusual?" Dan asked.

"I came in early to do the monthly inventory before I went to town to hit Costco," Sam answered. "Only car I saw parked alongside the road near the Willis place was a tan Jeep."

"You mean a white Jeep," Steve corrected.

"I thought it was tan, but the sun was just coming up so maybe I was wrong," she replied.

"A Wrangler Jeep?" Dan asked. "Only one around here with a white Jeep is Cliff. What would he be doing over there? He works in the other direction in town."

"No, this was more of an SUV, like a Cherokee. They've introduced so many models that lately I can't tell one from the other. It looked smaller than the old Cherokee though. Not like the one my Uncle Butch used to have." She shook her head to emphasize the point.

"Well, I saw a white SUV-type Jeep parked on the side of the road

35

near the Willis place but it was a government truck," Steve said. "Had a logo on the side. I think it was USGS. I heard they're measuring fault activity in the area again. But it was a quarter mile from Willis's road."

"Did you guys tell Thronson all this?" Dan looked from one to the other.

"Spinelli stopped in but he didn't ask any questions. He sat there muttering into his coffee mostly." Sam snickered. "Something put a bug up his butt."

Dan smiled but said, "He was probably thinking about suspects. Well, I better get going." As he headed for the door, Sam handed him another napkin. He looked at it. "You got something going on with my dog?"

"Working on it," she said and winked. Dan was not sure what that meant but was not going to pursue it.

CHAPTER 6 - WEDNESDAY, MAY 12TH

Dan had called Wally the previous evening and changed their plans to go to the powder coater to the afternoon. Their schedule changed frequently, but since it was only the two of them it was simple to coordinate. Arriving at the shop a bit early on Wednesday, Dan was well into his work when he noticed Wally was later than usual. He wondered if there was a mix-up in the plans after all. He couldn't call his uncle because the cell reception in the hills was practically nonexistent. Dan decided to give him another twenty minutes before walking over to the house to use a landline. Ten minutes later, Wally pulled up to the shop, got out of his truck muttering and slammed the door of his small Toyota 4x4. Even Syd walked out carefully to greet him because they could tell that something was wrong.

"What's up, Uncle?"

"That scrawny-assed little jerk," he sputtered. "If he didn't have on that uniform, I'd—"

"Whoa, slow down there. Don't go all apoplectic on me. What happened?"

"Speedy is what happened. The little weasel was lying in wait for me this morning. Pulled me over. I wasn't speeding because I had the steel you asked me to pick up in the back of my truck. Son of a…" He set his ice chest down. "Couldn't get me for speeding, so he walks around my truck inspecting for anything he could find. Wrote me a fix-it ticket because one of the bolts was missing on the front license plate. I ought to shove that license plate right up—"

"Easy there, Papi. You're gonna blow a fuse." Dan tried to calm him down.

"That little jerk kept me there for a half an hour while he sat in his car and supposedly ran my license. I think he sat back there playing with himself. He gets off on throwing his authority around. I'll show him some authority."

"You better chill there, tough guy. He's about half your age, you know." Dan tried to break the tension with a joke. "And you might have to get him a stool to stand on to make it fair." Wally was just over six foot, and Spinelli was only five foot six.

Wally finally smiled. "We'd better warn Ed he's prowling around."

"I think he's a bit afraid of Ed, but you're right, we should warn him." Dan walked over to a bank of hardware bins. "What size bolt do you need for the license plate before we forget to fix it?"

As they were fixing the Toyota, Dan told Wally about making the video and spending all evening reviewing it. Dan was not sure why, but something still bothered him about the shop. Maybe the deputies took away some of the evidence, but the more he looked at the tape the stronger his feeling was something wasn't adding up. They decided to review the video together later.

They had just finished fixing the license plate and were heading toward the door of the shop when they heard the racket of someone crossing the cattle guard at the end of the driveway. A car that looked like an unmarked police car headed toward them. It was a nondescript gray, but the antenna and other paraphernalia gave it away. It parked in front of the shop and a middle-aged guy in a brown sports coat got out and waved at them.

"What now?" Dan moaned.

The balding detective, who had a bad comb-over, spoke up. "Are you Dan Williams?"

"What can I do for you?" Dan replied.

"Don't tell this bastard anything. I don't trust 'em," Wally said under his breath.

The detective was about Dan's height, with a slight paunch. His manner was easy-going. "Man, it's nice out here. Long way out, though."

"That's what keeps it nice," Dan replied, nodding his head in agreement. "Keeps out most of the riff-raff. The rest we sic the dogs on."

Syd came out of the shop and stood beside Dan. A low growl sounded in her throat. Dan snapped his fingers and the dog looked up, then sat beside her owner waiting to see what would happen next.

"I'm Detective Sanchez. Just need to ask you some routine questions to follow up on the Willis murder. Do you have time to talk?"

"I'd hate to make you drive all the way out here again. We can do it now. C'mon in the shop where we can sit down."

Dan shook Sanchez's hand and led him into the shop. They pulled up some chairs and sat down, with Syd staying between the stranger and her owner. "Syd, heel," Dan said in an annoyed tone. The dog's ears dropped as she moved to the side of Dan's chair.

"Can you give me your account of what happened the morning of Mr. Willis's murder?" he asked, keeping it as open-ended as possible.

Wally leaned forward between the two. "Is my nephew a suspect? If he is, shouldn't he have a lawyer?"

"Lieutenant Thronson seems to be fine with Mr. Williams's explanation about the hammer. I'm here to do the routine follow-up. But given we don't have any leads at this point, I'm not ruling anyone out yet," he stated matter-of-factly, unaffected by Wally's aggressive posture. "Not even you."

"Well…" Wally sat back in his seat.

Dan walked Sanchez through Willis's visit, relaying that Willis told Dan he slid his Jeep off the road and wanted to borrow some tools. That was the day before they found him. He explained he did not hear anything else until Ed came to get them to go over to Willis's house the morning of his death. "I asked him if he wanted me to help him with the Jeep, but he was a pretty independent old cuss," Dan finished up.

"Well, we've established he was killed early in the morning, between four and six. Where were you at that time?"

"Home."

"Can't rule you out then." Sanchez looked disappointed.

"Wait, that was the morning I stopped by and you were showing me Syd's trick, wasn't it?" Wally pointed at Syd. "I got there just before six and he was getting out of the shower. So that should eliminate him."

"It helps, but there is still enough time before that, technically, for him to get back from being at Willis's at four-thirty or so. But thanks, that wasn't in the report." He smiled at Wally. "What kind of tricks does Syd do?"

"Aw, I taught her to find my cell phone when I misplace it," Dan said dismissively. "But Uncle, I think that was Monday anyway."

Sanchez looked around the shop. "So, what kind of work do you do for Ed Wyatt? You got a pretty good machine shop here."

"Ed's my uncle on my mom's side. I help him with the ranch, and this is a side thing my Uncle Wally, and I have been growing the last couple years. Wally is from my dad's side of the family."

"You married? Can your wife vouch for you earlier?" Sanchez asked expectantly.

Dan looked down. "No. She died in a car wreck five years ago." A wave of pain still hit him every time he said it aloud.

"Sorry to hear that. Anything else you can add? Seen anything unusual, or any strangers in the area? Did Willis have any enemies?" He held his hands out palms up, almost as if begging for a clue.

"Willis had no enemies that I knew. He could be abrupt if he thought you were wasting his time, but I don't know of any run-ins with anyone up here," Dan said thoughtfully, shaking his head.

"Hell, if people were getting killed for being grumpy, I would have been dead a long time ago," Wally added.

Dan noted Sanchez laughed a little too quickly in response.

He handed them both cards. "Well, give me a shout if you think of anything. Thanks."

"Oh, Detective, Willis's son Chuck asked us to keep an eye on the place. He took his mom into town to stay with him. There's no problem with us cruising by once in a while is there?" Dan almost regretted saying it.

"As long as you only cruise past. I wouldn't go in the garage or the house. If you see anything, stay in your car and give us a call. It will complicate the hell out of things if you go poking around." He stood and shook their hands. "Thanks again for your time."

After he had pulled out of the driveway, Wally said, "I thought I taught you it's easier to get forgiveness than permission."

"I know, I know."

Wally looked at Syd. "Girl, you are definitely smarter than your owner. You can tell him, but you can't tell him much." The dog barked in agreement.

Later that evening they were at Dan's place watching the video he shot. Dan had watched it probably twenty times and was frustrated by the fact that though he saw nothing, a part of his brain told him something was there.

Wally sat back, relaxed, drinking a can of Coke. He agreed something was odd. "Show me the outside of the shop again."

Dan pulled up the second file containing the outside walk he recorded. About halfway through it, Wally jumped from the couch. "There. Stop it."

Dan complied.

"Now count the outside studs you can see on that wall." The outside of the shop resembled a redwood fence. It had four-by-four inch studs exposed to both inside and out every ten feet or so. Between them, sheets of T-111 siding completed the outside wall. Between the larger studs were two-by-fours used to hold the siding. "I count four. So if those are ten-foot sections, that means the garage is forty feet long."

"I get four, too."

"Now, go back to the inside and count."

Dan went to the other video file.

"I don't see the fourth one. The workbench wouldn't hide it, and there're no windows on that side," Wally said, scanning the screen intently.

Dan jumped in the commentary. "Look. If you count the two-by-fours running in between, there aren't enough."

"There's four feet unaccounted for. That's a false back wall." Wally pointed to the screen.

Dan looked again and came to the same conclusion. "How'd you get that so fast?"

"I may not be ed-u-ma-cated," he said, faking a redneck accent, "but I can count to ten."

"I've never noticed a closet or anything there." Dan tried to remember the times he'd been in Willis's shop/garage. "What the hell is back there?"

"I say we stop by there in the morning like Chucky asked and make sure no one's bothering anything." Wally started toward the door. "Now unless there is another major mystery you need me to solve right now, I'm gonna go home to my supper. That crazy old married lady I'm living with don't like it when I'm late."

Dan laughed. "See you in the morning. Tell Aunt Bobbi hi."

"Don't you go poking around there without me."

"I won't, I promise."

~ ~ ~ ~

In addition to his public embarrassment by Thronson, Spinelli also received a severe dressing down in Thronson's office when they got back to the station. He didn't understand it. Who did they think found the murder weapon? He deserved a commendation. Well, he would show Thronson. He spent most of the next two days up in the hills. One reward he did get was stopping that old smartass in the Toyota truck. He made the old fart sit and wait and could tell he was steaming mad but could do nothing. Who had the upper hand now? The only problem with spending time up in the hills was the spotty radio reception. If they needed him for something, he might not hear the call. He could get in trouble, but he was busy patrolling the area to see if he could get a break in the case. No information was forthcoming from sitting at Sam's Place. He was sure one of the dumb yokels would let something slip. So far, nothing.

He could almost taste how sweet it would be to bust the bossy old guy, Ed. He didn't want to risk stopping him without a good reason because the old fart was obviously volatile. He would not be surprised if the grump killed Willis in a fit of temper. His real hope was that he could catch the other redneck, Dan Williams, either on the Willis property or trying to cover his tracks. That would get him back in the good graces of the lieutenant. He could not believe Thronson did not arrest Williams, or at least take him in for questioning.

When he cruised past the Rockin' A, he saw no activity at either the shop or at the main house. He knew this was where Ed lived. The nephew, Dan, lived over near the base of Mt. Hamilton's east side somewhere; he wasn't exactly sure of the location.

Spinelli kept moving slowly down the road and was soon coming up on the turn-off to the Willis property. Turning down the dirt road, he flipped off his headlights. It was getting dark, but you could still see the dirt path. As he was passing a small camp where the hunting club parked their RVs, he noticed a light-colored SUV sitting at the entrance. Maybe if he caught them red-handed on the property he could regain his credibility. He turned off the engine, lowered the volume on the radio and disabled the interior lights to keep from giving himself away.

Easing his door closed, he moved as silently as possible toward the SUV. He had his full-sized MagLite in his left hand, and his right hand rested on his holster strap. He inched along, trying not to step on any twigs or make any noise. He cursed the squeaking of his utility belt, its leather-on-leather sounding loud in the country stillness. He never noticed it in the city.

He could hear nothing but crickets. There was no one in the SUV as far as he could tell. When he got to where he could see into the windows, he turned on his flashlight. There was nothing in the back seat. The front only contained a map of the area and what looked like a laptop computer bag. As he shined the light into the rear window to check out the cargo area, he heard the snap of a twig behind him. He turned to look, but his eyes had not readjusted after using the flashlight on the car. Before he could swing the beam in that direction, everything went black.

CHAPTER 7 - THURSDAY, MAY 13TH

Dan's Thursday morning started before daylight with Wally meeting him at his place. The Hawk's Nest property wrapped around the side of Mt. Hamilton, while the San Antonio Valley continued north. Dan loved the isolation and beauty of the small spread he called home. On a clear day, from his deck you could see across the Central Valley and get a glimpse of the Sierra Nevada range with its snow-capped mountains in the distance.

Wanting to get a look at the rear wall of Willis's shop, Dan decided to take the back way instead of the main road. He figured they could use the fire trails running through the hills to keep a lower profile while checking on the property. Of course, it took longer because of all the gates, but Dan possessed the keys that would get him through to the Willis property. Dan and Ed had keys because they had good relationships with all of the neighbors. Dan also did occasional contract work with his grader and bulldozer for the CDF crew when they were shorthanded, which seemed to be a lot lately. Because he was a contractor, he possessed a CDF key for emergencies.

The Rockin' A bordered almost two-thirds of the Willis land, and as friendly neighbors they always let each other pass through. They stopped several times, with Wally climbing out of the cab and opening and holding the gates while Dan drove through. Syd was happy in the bed of the four-wheel-drive Dodge Ram diesel, sticking her nose over the side of the bed to sniff all the wild and domestic animals they passed.

When Dan and Wally reached the top of the ridge that looked down on the Willis property, it was just getting daylight. The hills to the west were bathed in a brilliance of orange and yellow light reflected from the trees, while the valley floor below still cast long shadows. Dan stopped and took out his binoculars to see if there was any activity below.

"You see anything?" Wally asked. Dan handed him the binoculars, pointing at a spot near the main road on the far side of the little valley.

"Light-colored SUV pulling out onto the road. Might have been turning around but the direction looks like he came from Willis's. See if you can tell what color it is for sure." Dan put the Dodge in gear and started down the ridge.

"Could it be a sheriff's truck?" asked Wally as he tried to keep the binoculars steady. "If you don't take it easy on these bumps, I'm likely to lose these binoculars out the window here, big guy." Dan slowed a bit as his uncle lowered the glasses. "Nope, I couldn't tell, and now we've dropped below the trees."

Dan began inching the truck forward as Wally was getting into the cab after opening the gate to the Willis property. He shushed Wally as he slammed the door and settled into the seat.

"You're not trying to sneak up on somebody in a freaking diesel truck, are you? If you want, I can tie some tin cans to the rear bumper to drown out the engine noise."

Dan shook his head.

"We shoulda brought my quiet little Toyota if you wanted stealth mode."

"Stop being a smartass and look, Uncle." Dan pointed to the house. The back door was slightly ajar. The door's only lock was the handle. There was no deadbolt on the back door so it would have been the most accessible point of entry for whoever broke in. Dan stopped the truck and they sat staring at the open door.

"That detective said you could only drive by," his uncle reminded him.

"I know." Dan sat thinking for a minute, looking around the property. "You wait here."

46

It had rained the night before, so Dan could only see one set of footprints going to the porch steps. He didn't want to leave proof he had gotten out of his truck. Wally watched as Dan opened the door and jumped from the cab. Dan leapfrogged from a patch of grass to a large stone in the yard, then to a milk crate that was upside down over the top of a small plant to protect it from chewing rabbits. Once he regained his balance, it was an easy climb over the side of the tiny concrete porch, up and over the rail.

"Anyone here?" Dan called as he pushed the partially open door with his elbow and disappeared into the house. Inside, he could see nothing disturbed in the kitchen, which was the first room he entered.

"Hello, Betty?" he called as he crept into the living room and dining room. He had visited occasionally but did not know the house intimately. Everything seemed intact. He walked down the hallway toward the bedrooms. The master bedroom looked ready for an inspection. The bed was made, everything neatly put away. The only things out of place were a closet door partially open and a sweater sleeve hanging out the edge of a bureau drawer. Betty was a meticulous housekeeper, so that might indicate someone had gone through them.

When he got to the back bedroom the old man used as a study, it looked as if someone had tossed the room. He knew Willis kept it a bit cluttered, but this place was a wreck. Drawers hung open, papers scattered everywhere. He took a few pictures with his phone and retreated from the house.

He carefully positioned the door the way it had been and started his retreat over the obstacle course he had taken. Trying again not to leave any footprints, his attempt was successful until he slipped off the side of the small rock. "Shit," he cursed, climbing into the truck.

"I'm sorry, but I'm gonna have to take points off for that landing there, bud," Wally goaded. "So what'd you find?"

"Somebody was in there. Whoever broke in didn't mess with much except Willis's office. They tore it up looking for something. We should report this to Sanchez." He thought for a minute. "They might be able to catch the guy before he gets too far. The car turned in the direction of Livermore."

There were only three roads out of the hills. To the south, the Mt. Hamilton road went past the Lick Observatory then wound down to San Jose, about twenty-five miles away. The northern direction was Mines Road, stretching thirty-five miles to Livermore. The only other option was to head east near Sam's Place to Patterson, which was also about thirty-five miles. If they got to the sheriff and the CHP, it would be easy to cover all the exits.

"Do you want to check out the shop first?"

"Not if they are going to have a chance to catch him. We can't call from here since we're not supposed to be in there, so we should go to the Rockin' A to use the phone." Dan put the truck in gear, easing past the shop to get a close look at the rear wall.

"With no windows in the three sides, it makes it hard to tell from here," Wally observed, shifting in his seat. As soon as they cleared the shop and he looked forward, he did a double take. "Is anybody hunting up here nowadays?"

"Shouldn't be anyone up here. Why?"

"Look to the right there. Somebody is parked at the hunters' camp."

Dan continued to ease forward as he and Wally scanned the scene.

"Over behind that clump of bushes. I thought I saw something."

As the road bent to the right they got a better view of the camp. There, partially concealed behind a group of bushes, was a sheriff's car.

"Speedy's up to his tricks again." Disgust was thick in Wally's voice. "Ain't no sneakin' by him in this truck."

As Dan pulled up nearer the patrol car, there was no sign of

Spinelli. They turned in and pulled behind it. Suddenly, the car bounced up and down as it sat there.

"Holy crap. Did Speedy get lucky with some skank from Sam's Place last night?" Wally raised himself up trying to see into the rear seat of the patrol car.

"I don't see anybody." Dan put the truck in park, and as he stepped to the ground he could hear banging and saw the metal of the trunk lid bulge slightly from a blow inside. "Uncle, I think someone is locked in there," he said.

Dan and Wally cautiously approached the patrol car. The banging continued and they could hear someone yelling. When Dan recognized the voice as Deputy Spinelli, he couldn't keep from smiling. He looked at his uncle and mouthed the word Speedy, causing Wally to double over in laughter. Dan smacked his uncle's arm to get him to straighten up and quit laughing.

"Hang on. We're trying to get you out," Dan yelled. He nodded for Wally to check in the car. "Are the keys in the ignition?"

Wally looked and shook his head no. He still couldn't speak for fear of bursting out laughing.

Dan glanced down to see if the keys were on the ground. He raised his voice again. "Hold on, we're trying to find the keys." Then to Wally, "Hey, Uncle, see if there's a remote trunk release."

Wally sat in the driver's seat and looked around. "There is, but like most law enforcement, they disable it when the ignition is off because they keep equipment and rifles in the trunk. It's not opening."

"Whoever did this probably threw the keys somewhere, to slow anyone down when they found him." Dan turned toward his truck. "Syd."

The dog, curiously watching the spectacle from the bed of the truck, immediately leaped over the side and came to sit at Dan's feet.

"Find the keys, Syd, find the keys."

Wally, who was climbing out of the patrol car, looked at Dan skeptically and watched the dog as she began to work. Syd started in close circles near the vehicle and ran in an ever-widening circle through the bushes and trees with her nose to the ground. Wally looked at Dan as Syd disappeared into one of the clusters of shrubs. "If she scares up a rabbit, she's gone."

Dan smiled.

When the dog was about thirty yards out from the patrol car on the driver's side, she let out an excited little yip. Both Dan and Wally looked in the direction of the sound. Within seconds, Syd came prancing out of the bushes with a set of car keys in her mouth and dropped them at Dan's feet. Dan bent down and hugged the dog, petting her briskly.

"Good dog. Good Syd." Picking up the keys, he turned to the trunk.

As soon as the trunk was open, Wally could see tactical boots flailing in the air and heard a high-pitched scream.

"Get me the hell out of here!"

Sure enough, it was Spinelli, his hands handcuffed above his head to the trunk hinge so he couldn't reach the truck release. The front of his pants was damp where he'd wet himself, and he was mad as a hornet.

"Calm down, calm down. We have to find the handcuff keys now." Dan finally got him to stop kicking.

"There's a set on the car key ring." Spinelli's voice broke as he spoke.

Dan took the keys out of the trunk lid and found the handcuff key. He released one wrist and handed Spinelli the keys so he could unlock the other cuff. Dan helped him out of the trunk, careful to avoid the soiled trousers.

As soon as Spinelli's feet hit the ground he squirmed away from Dan. Surprisingly, he still had his gun, probably only because whoever locked him in the trunk situated him so he couldn't reach it with his hands cuffed over his head. He backed away from Dan on shaky legs and immediately pulled his service weapon.

"Very funny, you son of a bitch." He slammed the trunk and motioned with the gun for Wally to move beside Dan. "Both of you put your hands on the trunk of the car."

"Whoa, whoa, whoa. We just saved your ass and you pull a gun on us?" Wally couldn't believe his eyes. "You're losing it, Speedy. This here is some serious shit."

Dan could see Wally was getting angry. "Uncle, calm the hell down." Looking at Spinelli, he asked, "How long have you been in there?"

"Hilarious, asshole, since you're the one who put me there." He stepped forward and closed a cuff around Dan's right wrist and the other on Wally's left. "Now get in the backseat. And just be glad I don't haul your ass down the hill in the trunk."

"I haven't seen you since the other day at Willis's. You look like you took a blow to the head Spinelli. Seriously, you're not thinking straight." Dan tried to reason with him. "Why would I throw you in a trunk and come back and let you out?"

"You are a suspect in the Willis murder, and you two are the only ones up here with a grudge against me," Spinelli said as he waved the gun trying to get them to move. "You're the only ones with motive."

"How did someone get the jump on you?"

Spinelli thought for a moment. "I was checking out a vehicle that was here. It was dark and they snuck up on me," he said, sounding unsure.

"What kind of vehicle? It wasn't mine. I haven't been up here at all until now," Dan protested.

"I…I don't remember." Spinelli raised his left hand to the back of his head, felt the bump and winced. "Get in the car, before I shoot you. You two should not be on this property anyway. It is a crime scene. You're a suspect, and your idiot uncle there is probably pissed

51

because I gave him a ticket."

Dan and Wally walked around to the passenger side rear door then Dan sat down and scooted across the seat. The back door was still open on the driver's side from when Wally was looking for the keys, and Dan was tempted to keep sliding out the other way. With Wally attached to him, he didn't think this was a good idea.

"Spinelli, we might have seen the guy who did this to you. Somebody was leaving when we came up over the ridge. Maybe we can help you. We need to get your guys to block the roads. Does your radio work up here?"

Spinelli shook his head. "I don't have the big whip antennae you need."

"Well, we'll have to go to the Rockin' A to call from there. We still have time to catch this guy." Dan could tell nothing was registering. "It was a light-colored SUV." A slight look of recognition crossed Spinelli's face like he was trying to recall something, then he shook his head and closed the passenger door.

"Nice try, asshole. Now shut up, you're giving me a headache." He was backing up so he could keep his weapon on the two suspects as he swung around to the other side of the car. Both Wally and Dan locked eyes with him. Suddenly, Syd was behind Spinelli. As Spinelli took another step back, he fell over the dog. His head slammed backward into a branch on the ground causing him to reach up with both hands to cover the back of his skull. The pain and the motion of his hands caused him to release the gun, which tumbled away.

"God that hurts," Spinelli moaned as he checked his hand for blood. The blow had landed on the tender spot where he had been knocked unconscious the night before.

Before the dazed deputy recovered, Syd leaped over him and picked up the key ring in her mouth. The dog ran about twenty yards away and turned to look at Dan. Spinelli started kicking his legs again in frustration, then sat up trying to figure out what happened. Spinelli scrambled around on his knees looking for his service weapon. Syd trotted away a few more feet.

"Stinking mutt." Spinelli finally found the gun, but it was sticking in the ground barrel first, filled with dirt. So Spinelli stood, spun and headed for the passenger side of the car.

"Run, Syd!" Dan shouted, seeing that Spinelli was reaching for the shotgun strapped to the dash of the patrol car. The dog disappeared into the bushes before Spinelli could get his upper body back out of the vehicle.

Spinelli racked a round into the chamber and brought it up, pointing to where the dog had been. "Damn it. Call that damned dog back here."

Wally looked at Spinelli and shook his head. "You are the dumbest person I have ever met. I hope you do take us to jail now so I can tell all of your buddies how you were disarmed and disabled by a dog." He started laughing. "I don't think Speedy is a good name for you at all. Maybe we'll have to change it to Deputy Dumbass from now on." Wally snickered to himself and looked at Spinelli, shaking his head.

"Okay, then we'll take your truck. I think you'll be comfortable in the bed." Spinelli sneered at both of them.

"Good luck with that," Dan joined in, angry that Spinelli pulled a shotgun on his dog. "The keys are in my pants pocket. And even with one hand, if you come close enough to get these keys, I am going to beat the living snot out of you. So, come on in here, Sunshine. I'd like to see you try."

Spinelli was still woozy from the blow to the head and did not feel up to challenging the bigger man. The deflated deputy leaned against the front fender of the cruiser, his head bowed, arms dropped straight to his side. The end of the shotgun barrel was in his right hand.

Wally looked over at Dan. "I think he's crying." They could see his shoulders shake slightly.

Dan sat there a minute, giving Spinelli time to compose himself. "Hey, Spinelli." No response. "I'll make you a deal." He saw the deputy's head turn slightly toward them. "I'll let you take me in if you turn my uncle loose."

Spinelli sat there a few minutes weighing his options. He raised his head up to the sky as if to say why me? Finally, he came and sat in the front passenger seat, looking exhausted and beaten. "Okay, I'll turn your uncle loose if you promise me he won't try to stop me from taking me in." He looked from one to the other. Both nodded. "Call your damned dog."

Dan whistled and Syd came shooting out of the bushes then ran to the rear door where he was sitting. Motioning in the general direction, he said, "Get the keys, Syd." The dog shot off and returned proudly bringing the keys to her master, who held onto them and looked at Spinelli. "No more threats?"

"No threats, I just want to get out of this godforsaken place." Spinelli looked like he was ready to cry again.

Dan unlocked their wrists from the handcuffs and passed the keys to Wally. Wally had to reach out the passenger window to hand them to Spinelli because of the cage behind the front seat. Scratching Syd's ears with his free hand, Dan said, "Good girl. Who's the wonder dog?"

Now that he had the keys, Spinelli motioned for Wally to exit the car. Before he got out of the cruiser, Wally looked over at Dan and stuck out his hand.

"I'm gonna need your truck keys."

Dan nodded toward the truck. "They're in the ignition." Then he winked at his uncle.

Spinelli looked at him and shook his head, then put the cuffs back in his belt.

"Don't forget to call in about the break-in, Spinelli." Uncle Wally said, then turned and walked to the truck, told Syd to mount up and backed it out of Spinelli's way. Spinelli backed up the patrol car, then pulled up beside Wally, rolling down his window.

"By the time I get within range of my radio, they'll likely be long gone," Spinelli said and shrugged his shoulders. "But I'll try."

Uncle Wally followed them to the road but turned right toward the Rockin' A. He stopped at the house to let Ed know where Dan would be. Ed was planning on going into town, so agreed to bring Dan home, freeing Wally to get some work done on one of the projects due soon.

~ ~ ~ ~

Wally worked in the shop until about lunchtime. He kept going over the day's events in his head. He noticed Syd would get up from her bed in the corner and stare at Dan's truck every once in a while. Then, with a sigh, she would go and lie down.

"It's okay, girl." The dog moved her eyes to look over at him without raising her head. Wally didn't think Syd believed him. As he sat chewing the sandwich he'd brought for lunch, he suddenly looked over at the dog and said, "C'mon, Syd, let's take a ride." Syd perked up immediately. As he was leaving, Wally grabbed a sawed-off rake handle used to prop open the side door of the shop. It was about three feet long, not much of a weapon, but it was something.

He figured that Deputy Dipshit was currently occupied so he wouldn't have to worry about him. Now would be the safest time to do some snooping of his own. So, he headed to the Willis property using Dan's Dodge and figured he'd have a look around.

Wally parked beside Willis's shop and counted the main studs and the distance between them again to make sure his calculations from the video were correct. Taking Dan's video camera from the truck's console, he knew Dan would want him to record everything. Climbing out of the cab, he walked behind the building. Willis built it into a hill; the rear of the property was higher than the front. When he looked closer at the base of the building, the concrete looked like it extended into the embankment. *Maybe they made an extra wide footing for strength?*

Wally walked around to the front, glanced at the small piece of police tape still stuck to a staple from when they removed it and went into the shop. Just seeing the yellow strip brought back the image of Willis on the floor and caused a shiver to go through him. There was a smell of gasoline and grease. As he approached the back wall, he again counted the main studs and the smaller studs in between. There had to be a false wall. The trick was to find out how to access it. He looked at the workbench built into the wall. Pulling on it didn't seem to budge it at all. He tried reaching over the bench and knocking on the wall to see if he could hear any hollow sections. They all sounded alike, so the space behind it was either filled or it was all open space.

Wally took a flashlight to look for scrape marks on the floor that movement might cause but could see none. He cursed the fact he left his new glasses, the ones without all the scratches, in his truck at Dan's place this morning. Seeing clearly with this old pair required him to kneel.

To his left, there was a black, full-sized tool chest about five feet tall. It was an expensive-looking unit, and it was full of high-quality tools that looked almost new. Every drawer was neat and clean. Wally tried to move the tool chest. Even though it had wheels, it felt anchored to the floor. When he shined the flashlight down to see if the wheels were locked, he noticed round steel bars extending from the bottom of the toolbox into holes drilled in the floor at each corner. The holes in the concrete had a steel collar around the top of them to keep the cement from chipping. *No wonder it felt bolted.*

Someone added this locking mechanism to the chest because it was not a standard setup. The two bars on each end were attached to a handle. Wally noticed a button on the handle. When he pressed it, the button released the bars so the end of the toolbox was free to move. He grabbed the bar on the other end and released it. The chest now rolled across the concrete floor.

Wally, feeling he was onto something, looked at the wall behind it. It appeared the same as the rest of the wall. Pegboard covered the entire area with various hand tools hanging from it. Using his flashlight to peer behind the pegboard, he could see plywood on the other side of the studs.

One of the sections of pegboard was a different size than the others. It also stuck out a bit instead of lying flush with its adjacent panel. That was interesting. Wally pushed, but it seemed secure. He grabbed one of the hangers in the pegboard and pulled. Nothing. When he shoved to the right, however, it slid effortlessly on a narrow track.

He knocked on the plywood behind the open panel of pegboard, then pushed on it. It didn't move. Shining his flashlight, he noticed a small hole in the left side of the plywood. It looked like a natural knothole in the oak grain of the plywood, but it was big enough for the end of your finger. Shining the light into the hole revealed nothing. Wally stuck his finger in the hole and pulled to his right. The plywood panel slid into a pocket door. He was in.

Wally shoved his upper body through the open panel and shined the flashlight around. "What the hell?" he muttered. The fake wall was hiding a descending staircase. *But where could it go?* There was no basement in the garage.

Remembering the mission he was on, he stepped back and took out the video camera. He recorded the opening, the panel with its catches and hinges, and filmed the toolbox with its custom locking mechanism and the holes on the floor, narrating as he went. Wally leaned back in through the hidden door, shining the flashlight, and captured the staircase. He wished there was a way to mount the camera on his head or shoulder.

Wally ducked through the opening. He could stand up but felt something like a spider web touch his forehead. He jerked his head back wiping his face and shined the flashlight up. A string hung from a bare overhead light bulb. He pulled it and the light came on. He could see nothing down the staircase except an opening at the bottom left. That should be outside the shop.

As Wally started down the stairs, he noticed an electrical conduit ran along the ceiling of the staircase down to the room. When he reached the bottom stair, he saw a light switch. Wally hit the switch, then looked through the doorway. What he saw amazed him. In front of him was a long narrow room. He estimated it to be about forty feet long. Remembering the camera, he brought it up to film. As he was panning around the room, it occurred to him this was a shipping container Willis had buried in the ground behind his shop. *Why?*

The room had three sections. The first area contained a tiny sink like in an older RV, complete with running water, a few cabinets, and a coffee maker. Beyond it was an old brown recliner that looked as if it had taken the shape of Willis's body from years of use. A wooden desk sat beside it, complete with a computer and covered in papers. On the wall above the desk was a map of South America with different colored pushpins and some cryptic notes written on it. A whiteboard on wheels sat against the wall. When Wally pulled the board out to look at it, the side facing the wall contained some math calculations and more cryptic notes. At the rear of the room were a mixture of bookshelves of dark wood and a few metal racks loaded with books. Talk about a man cave. But this one was designed for a scientist.

Wally wondered if this was a bomb shelter Willis converted, or if he built it himself. If so, why would he need such a place? Continuing to record, he walked around the room. The books on the shelves were related to physics, nuclear physics, history of Argentina, and there was a separate section on World War II history. He made sure to capture the papers on the desk along with a three-ring binder. They appeared to be photocopies of documents in German, with handwritten notes in English in the margins. What the heck was Willis researching?

As Wally turned to record the entrance, he saw a red light above the door and wondered why it was illuminated. As he walked among the rows of bookshelves, he noticed another small whiteboard on the rear wall of the room. It seemed an odd place for it, in a location not easily accessible. His curiosity made him look behind it, where he found a small door or hatch about waist high. He removed the whiteboard and recorded it, and still holding the camera in his left hand, tried the latch. The handle turned freely and it swung open, but the space behind it was dark. *Perhaps it was an escape tunnel.*

He had been down here long enough, so was not inclined to explore further and turned to leave. The red light made him nervous. Since Willis was retired from Lawrence Livermore, where they did work on nuclear bombs and radiation, Wally was afraid he tripped some booby trap mechanism. Wally tried to tell himself his imagination was getting away from him. Still, someone could discover him if he stayed too long. Moving past the desk, Wally decided to grab the binder and take it with him. Under it was a manila folder, which he also grabbed without looking at it. He had plenty to show Dan.

He left the room, slowly making one more pan as he stepped out. He turned off the overhead lights and climbed the stairs. As he was exiting, he noticed everything on the door and the toolbox operated so they could lock from the inside. The design would allow you to be in the room with no indications of occupancy in the garage. Perhaps it was a safe room.

Wally stepped out of the false wall and slid the plywood pocket door and the pegboard closed. In his hurry to escape any booby trap, he did not notice the top of the pegboard did not stay securely in place. He rolled the toolbox in place and pushed the handles down to secure it.

As he walked through the shop, he rerecorded everything, to compare it with the original recording and determine if someone disturbed anything. He went to the garage door and popped his head out to see if anyone was around. It looked deserted outside, so he exited and closed the door. He hurriedly left the property, feeling like a burglar who stole the crown jewels. He was a genuinely honest man, and his guilt would be evident to anyone who saw him. His goal was to get to Dan's shop so he could hide the binder and the file folder.

~ ~ ~ ~

The man standing on the ridge watched through binoculars as a figure exited the garage, skulking to his truck carrying a blue binder and some files. The observer couldn't tell from this distance which person was leaving. It seemed everyone in the hills wore the same ball cap and jeans. He did recognize the truck, though, so he had a pretty good idea who it was taking something from the Willis property. The observer didn't worry about being seen, as he was some distance away and surrounded by bushes. He was also a small target, having walked to the ridge on foot, leaving his Jeep by the road. The SUV was hidden behind some bushes where no one would notice it. He was curious about what the figure was carrying. There were no binders or file cabinets in the shop when he searched it. He would have to take another look.

CHAPTER 8 - THURSDAY AFTERNOON

Ed drove to the Santa Clara County Sheriff's offices in San Jose wondering what would happen next. He knew Dan could never do such a thing but wondered how he got himself into a position where the deputy arrested him. The boy had a temper if pushed too far and could be stubborn if he felt he was wronged or slighted. The boy. Ed chuckled to himself. Dan was in his mid-thirties. He was smart as a whip and could quickly master anything that captured his interest. Ed had watched as Dan took up machining just a few years ago and was already earning a good portion of his income from it. All this was accomplished using a secondhand collection of mills and lathes he picked up for next to nothing. The kid would drag them into the shop, repair the machines and use them to add to his arsenal of tools. Dan was the son he'd always wanted, and Ed was glad he stuck around after Janet died.

Ed had quite a few errands to run while in town and tried to steel himself for the hassles bound to come. He was not looking forward to going through the bureaucratic process of bailing Dan out, which would likely take most of his day.

Ed walked into the sheriff's office and the desk sergeant directed him to the kitchen. As Ed approached, he heard Dan speaking. He found Dan sitting with a group of deputies telling stories that had them in stitches.

"So then my Uncle Ed steps in front of us and says, 'Son, if you pull that gun, I have four witnesses who will testify the reason they found it up your ass—'" Dan stopped speaking when he saw Ed approaching.

Ed hoped Dan was not making things worse by telling stories to the deputies that would further antagonize Spinelli. The last thing they needed was someone in the sheriff's office with a vendetta. Not that they did anything illegal, but as Spinelli did with Wally, he could keep poking around until he found something that allowed him to charge you. Ed was shocked when he turned the corner into the kitchen and saw Spinelli was part of the group and was laughing along with the others.

"What the heck is going on here?" Ed looked alternately from Dan to the group. Dan was sitting on the top of a chair back with his left foot in the seat, his right leg holding most of his weight. He had a bottle of Dr. Pepper in his hand and a big smile on his face.

"Oh, we're just telling tales. It took you long enough to get here." Dan grinned at Ed.

"Well, I figured you'd be getting a cavity search about now." The deputies laughed. "Didn't know I was on a schedule."

"We cleared everything up. On the long ride down, I told Deputy Spinelli that Sanchez gave me permission to watch the property as long as I didn't disturb anything and took a witness with me. I let him know someone broke into the house. He also remembered it wasn't my truck he was checking out when he got hit. Once we got here and he confirmed everything with Sanchez, we waited for you. We've already filled out the reports so we're taking a coffee break."

Spinelli spoke up. "Yeah, we reached a kind of understanding. I apologized to Dan for overreacting, but I was so mad about being locked in the trunk I wasn't thinking straight. We decided to share information."

"I was educating the fellas here on dealing with the folks up in the hills." Dan looked at the group and then over at Ed.

"Yeah, I'll bet you were. Well, come on, professor, I've got errands to run." He nodded to the group. "Good to see you, fellas." He turned and headed for the door, with Dan rushing to untangle his legs from the chair and catch up.

After spending most of the rest of the day running Ed's errands they decided to grab some dinner before heading up the hill. As they sat at a table in a small Mexican restaurant in a strip mall eating chips and enjoying cold Modelo Especial, Ed finally broached the subject.

"You think it was a good idea to be telling embarrassing stories about Spinelli to his coworkers?"

Dan shrugged his shoulders. "We kinda bonded today. Between being locked in the trunk and outsmarted by a dog, he had kind of hit rock bottom. So I took a chance on the drive down the hill and opened up to him about what I knew. I think he could finally see I wasn't the enemy."

"Still, you don't want to make him look bad in front of his peers."

"No, he started the story. I was just clarifying. You'll laugh. He described you as about six foot five. He said he almost shit his pants." Dan grinned. "He's not a bad guy. Good sense of humor, but still trying to prove himself in a new job. I think he might have gained some points by how gruff you acted when you picked me up."

Ed laughed and shook his head. "Six-five. I used to be six foot one, but old age and arthritis took at least two inches from me."

~ ~ ~ ~

Wally was going stir-crazy sitting on the information he'd found at Willis's secret hideout. He was pacing the floor of the shop, opening and closing the binder and the files repeatedly, hoping something would jump out that made some sense. Most of it was in German and indecipherable to him. Even the few things in English were written in some type of code, so he was not sure of the subject. He wished Ed would get home with Dan so he could hand the burden off.

One thing he did recognize was the Reichstag Eagle insignia—the eagle holding a wreath with a Swastika in the middle—used by the

Nazis during World War II. That symbol was present throughout the documents. He didn't think Willis was old enough to be a Nazi. *What in the world was he doing with papers like these? How did he get his hands on such information?* Stamped all over the pages were the words Top Secret. So it must have come from within the US after they got them from the Nazis. Willis had some dark, scary stuff in his possession.

There was no cell signal to call Dan. Plus, if Dan were locked up, he would not have his phone on him. Ed had not returned yet, so Wally was not comfortable entering Ed's house to use the landline, even though he was sure Ed wouldn't mind. Wally doubted the place was locked, but you don't go into a man's home uninvited. He was not sure where Margaret was, but her car was gone. Someone had to be back soon to feed the animals. Wally also needed to get home because his wife, Bobbi, would worry if he was too late for dinner. He gave up around seven, already past his dinnertime. He would have to call Bobbi as soon as he got a cell signal to tell her he was running late.

Wally needed to go Dan's place to switch vehicles before heading home because he left his truck there this morning. He decided to close up the shop, but as he was starting out the rolling door, stopped and went back inside. After everything that happened this week, Wally did not want to leave the documents in the shop unprotected. Syd stood watching him curiously as he went inside. Picking up the binder and the manila folder, he looked out the door, exited, closed it, and trotted over to Dan's truck. On the drive down to Dan's place Wally kept an eye on his mirrors to ensure no one was following because he was so worried about taking the documents.

By the time he went to Hawk's Nest to switch to his truck, feed Syd, and make it an area where his phone had a signal, he would be very late for dinner. The documents sitting on the passenger seat weighed heavily on his mind. After seeing that symbol on the pages, he did not want to even be close to them but wasn't sure what to do with them. Knowing he must keep them safe, he looked around at Dan's place. Walking into the small shop at Hawk's Nest, he saw Dan's dirt bike sitting on a plastic milk crate. He took the bike off of the container, lifted it up and put the documents underneath it. He grabbed a repair manual that was on the bench and placed it on top of the binder. Putting the milk crate back in place, he hoisted the bike on it, using it as a center stand. Hidden in plain sight would have to do for now.

When he got to civilization and a cell signal, he called and left a message for Dan to call him. Then Wally called his wife to let her know he'd be late. He told her about Dan getting arrested but not about the documents. No need to worry her.

~ ~ ~ ~

The long day in San Jose and the drive home had exhausted Ed. He enjoyed spending time with Dan and having dinner, however, by the time they got back to the Rockin' A it was pushing nine o'clock. He hurried to feed the animals with Dan's help.

Rather than go through the trouble of having Ed drive him home, which was about twelve miles away, Dan used one of the older ranch trucks parked by the barn. It isn't far as the crow flies, but since it was on a dirt road off the main highway about two miles, the round trip took close to an hour.

Ed finally settled down to watch some television before going to bed. Margaret was visiting her sister for a few days. Suddenly Rounder was raising a ruckus outside. Rounder would typically give a bark if someone pulled onto the ranch property, not like the noise he was making now, which sounded as if he was really after something. He worried about coyotes setting a trap for Rounder. They will often lure a dog by getting him to chase one of them, and the pack would jump the unsuspecting animal.

Ed grabbed a rifle from the gun safe by the front door and headed out to check. He could hear Rounder barking and headed in the direction of the barn and the shop. The dog moved at first like it was investigating, head and tail up, easing forward at a trot. Suddenly, Ed saw the figure of a man come out of the dark doorway of the shop and take off at a sprint toward the barn behind it. He was going to use the side of the building as cover. Rounder saw him at the same time and took off running toward the barn, tail out straight, head down and ears back. His bark indicated he meant business now.

"Hey! Who's there?" Ed shouted and took off at a run.

As Rounder got to the corner of the barn where the tall figure disappeared, the man ran from the opposite corner, up the short hill to the road. Rounder paused to look at Ed when he came past the other side of the barn. The hesitation was just enough to let the figure reach his car on the edge of the road. Ed heard the engine start and tires squeal as it took off. The driver did not turn on the lights, but standing on the edge of the hill Ed could see the brake lights as the SUV rounded the next corner. He couldn't tell the color, only that it was a light-colored SUV, possibly a Jeep Cherokee.

Ed scratched the dog's ears and patted his side when he came up to him. "Good boy. Good Rounder. He won't be coming back tonight." They both watched and listened as the vehicle disappeared down the road.

CHAPTER 9 - FRIDAY, MAY 14TH

The sun was barely peeking over the horizon the next morning when Dan heard a vehicle pull up in his front yard. Hawk's Nest was perched high on the east side of the Diablo Range, so Dan usually saw the sun before anyone. He heard Syd give a wuffling bark, which meant it was someone she knew. Dan hoped it was just some hunters or someone from the Rockin' A going to check on cows. He heard the front door open, and before his eyes could adjust to the morning sun coming through the window, Wally was at the foot of his bed.

"Where were you all day yesterday? I waited until after seven for your lazy butt to get back," Wally chided his nephew.

Dan didn't answer.

"Did you and Speedy have a good time yesterday?" Wally peppered him.

Dan grunted.

"Get your ass up. We got things to talk about."

"Leave me alone you crazy old goat. I had a rough day yesterday," Dan whined as he threw a pillow.

Wally caught it and began to hit Dan with it. Syd jumped on the bed to join in the fun.

"Get him, Syd," Dan commanded. Syd grabbed the pillow with her teeth and, trying to position herself for leverage, planted her back paws on Dan's stomach. Dan rolled off the bed. "Watch the feet, girl. You were a little too close to the package."

"Oh, good. You're up." Wally smiled down at him.

"You're an asshole, Uncle." Dan stood up and staggered into the bathroom for a hot shower.

Twenty minutes later he came into the kitchen, where Wally was enjoying a cup of coffee. Dan was dressed in jeans and pulling on a

67

shirt while carrying his socks and work boots. "What's so danged important that got Sleeping Beauty out of his bed this early?" Dan slapped his uncle on the arm. "You never get here before eight o'clock."

Wally poured Dan a cup of coffee and told him to sit down. For the next hour, he went over the previous day's events that took place after Dan and Spinelli left for San Jose. Wally was talking excitedly and at one point ran out of the house. Dan hesitantly followed him to the small shop. When he saw Wally grab his dirt bike, he became concerned, until he noticed the documents hidden under the milk crate. Wally grabbed the binder and began going through the pages until he finally thrust it at Dan.

"Look at this. It's all in German. I was confused until I saw the Nazi insignia, then I got really concerned. What was Willis doing with these?" His voice went up a full octave and he was talking so fast the only word Dan was sure he heard was Nazi.

When they walked into the house, he tried to slow his uncle down and go over it. It was too much information to process this early. Dan, who didn't like coffee and rarely drank it, started on his third cup.

"Okay, first, let's take a look at the video you shot yesterday so I can see what you're talking about." Dan started a to-do list on some note cards he dug out of a drawer in the kitchen to help keep his thoughts organized. "Then, I want to go take a look at this room. Maybe it will give us some hint of what Willis was doing, or was trying to do."

Wally nodded agreement.

"We're going to have to go to the police with this, but it's probably more of a federal issue and I know I don't want to play with those guys," Dan concluded.

"No, they have no sense of humor whatsoever," Wally agreed. "Are we probably screwed by what we've already found?"

Dan thought for a bit before answering. They were primarily trying to figure out who was on the property, and they'd been asked to watch the property by the owner, or at least her son. They had no idea of any motive for the murder. There was no indication the stuff Wally found was even legitimate. But if it was not real, why in the world did Willis have a hidden room? The more they dug into this, the less anything made sense.

"I don't think we're in trouble yet. But we can't sit on this information too long without reporting it. The sheriff will hit us with impeding an investigation at least." He grabbed his pack of note cards and headed for the door. "Let's go to the shop and see if we can make sense of it. A guy's stopping by to look at the flat track motorcycle frame I have for sale."

They packed up and headed for the shop. On the way, Dan's brain was swirling. It was hard to believe things were normal only four days ago. When they got to the shop, Dan unloaded everything, turned around and pulled down the roll-up door. Assuming they were leaving again, Syd got up from her bed.

Dan took out the index cards and a marker and began writing frantically. He grabbed a roll of masking tape and started putting the cards on the door using a strip of tape. He put a timeline at the very bottom, beginning with Monday. Each day was a column on the door. He then arranged things they knew or observed in the rows based on the day they learned of them.

As he wrote out the cards and put them on the timeline, he repeated the facts they knew so far. "So we know that Tuesday is when Willis was killed and that Sam saw a tan SUV early Tuesday near Willis's. So did Steve. Can you think of anything else on Tuesday?" Dan asked Wally.

Wally thought for a minute and shook his head.

In the Wednesday column, Dan started a row. "Wednesday was the day Spinelli gave you a ticket, and we know he was locked in the trunk later that evening." Turning to Wally, he asked, "Anything for Wednesday?"

Wally wrinkled his brow. "Wasn't that the day we talked to Sanchez?"

"Yep." Dan wrote out a card for talking to Detective Sanchez. "Okay, what about yesterday?" Dan created a Thursday column. "That was the morning we went by to check on the Willis place and saw the light-colored SUV." Another card went on the board. "We found the house broken into, and then we found Spinelli in the trunk."

Wally grabbed two cards, wrote something and posted them in the Thursday column. "That was when Spinelli took you downtown and I found the hidden room." They stood back and looked. "Oops, forgot one." Wally grabbed another card, hiding what he wrote on it. Smiling, he stepped up and added it to the Thursday column—Syd outsmarts Spinelli.

"Uncle, be nice," Dan chided. They both considered the cards again.

"That's all we know?" Wally sounded disappointed.

"Let's look at your video." Dan grabbed the recorder and set it on the table where they could both see the small screen. It started abruptly, showing the toolbox and the hidden entrance. "I've been in there at least a dozen times and never noticed how the toolbox was anchored. I probably would have thought it was to secure it. Good eye, Uncle."

The recording showed the stairway and the entrance to the room. Wally and Dan both sat forward staring intently at the screen.

"When the heck did he build this?" Dan asked. "I would have thought he would come to me for the digging and electrical."

"He probably brought in outsiders on purpose so no one local would know what he was doing."

As the camera scanned the bookshelves, the back hatch came into view Dan pointed at the screen. "Where does that go?"

"I did a brief check. It wasn't locked and opened to a dark space. I assumed it was an escape tunnel. I was down there so long I thought I'd better get out of Dodge." He told Dan about the red light over the doorway and how it made him nervous not knowing what it meant.

"That was the smartest thing you did all day." He elbowed his uncle. "You shouldn't have gone in there by yourself."

"Hey, screw you, kid," he said in mock anger. "You ain't the boss of me."

Dan added another index card to Thursday—Documents in German. He returned to the video that showed the inside of the building.

"Look, there." Dan pointed at the screen. "Someone has searched the shop again. Willis always kept those rags folded. As soon as he used one, he would put it in that blue bin for laundry. Those are messed up, not in a neat stack. I remember they were folded in the earlier recording." He looked at his uncle. "I recall thinking how anal Willis was."

"You could learn a thing or two from him, you know," Wally joked. He looked around Dan's shop. It was pretty organized. There were a few tools out of place, but it wasn't bad. "Maybe the detective moved some of the things around during his review of the scene."

"Hey, if anything is out of place around here, it's because of you. I'm always looking for things after you leave." It was a standing argument between the two and they both laughed. Dan filled out a card about the shop being searched and put it on their improvised timeline.

"I think we both need to take a look at this room, what do you say?"

"Let's go." At the word "go" Syd jumped up from her bed and headed toward the door. She was in Dan's truck before the shop door closed.

"I'm gonna take my truck so we can head out from there instead of coming back." Wally jumped in his truck and they headed toward the Willis property.

~ ~ ~ ~

The news of Willis's death was frustrating for Albert. He had set up his surveillance cameras early Tuesday morning to monitor the old man, then left to enjoy a few days in Napa while in the area.

When he saw it on the local news, he rushed back to find out what was going on. There was so much activity around the Willis property he was not able to complete his work. Albert did not want to get tangled in the investigation, so decided to risk leaving the cameras in place to monitor things.

Every time he'd gone onto the property, someone had shown up, and he'd needed to go before being discovered. With Willis now gone, Albert had to make sure he knew what the police, and others, were taking from the old man's property. Some of it could be critical to his mission. He couldn't let it fall into the wrong hands. Today he was merely trying to get close enough to extend his wireless network. He initially installed battery-powered cameras at various places on the property allowing him to watch the target. By setting up the Wi-Fi network he did not have to visit each of the cameras to download the data, he only needed to get close enough to reach a Wi-Fi signal. Even that was difficult, and this morning he had to park several miles away and hike into the area.

Man, I'm going to have to start jogging again, Albert admonished himself. The hike in the hills was leaving him breathless.

An extender was the latest addition to his arsenal. Typically he could use a cell phone signal and sit in his hotel to watch a target. The lack of cell signal in the hills required him to take more chances.

Why did this guy have to live in the middle of nowhere? He shook his head as his phone continued to display the No Service message.

He hid the extender in the crook of a tree and only stayed long enough to determine that it was successfully broadcasting. Albert pulled out his phone again and connected via the Wi-Fi interface. Once back in his truck, he began to upload the data to his laptop.

Yay, the extender works perfectly. Albert loved it when his gadgets saved him time and effort. Now he could sit in his truck a safe distance away.

He started with the camera mounted to monitor the power the Willis property was using. The power reading would give him a good indication whether Willis was experimenting. You cannot do the type of experimentation he suspected the old physicist might be doing without a significant increase in power consumption. The recording showed almost no power use over the past week. That either indicated he was still in the literary research phase or had an alternate means of generating power. Albert did not see any solar panels on the property, and if Willis had generators, they would have created a noise signature. No, he assured himself, it was good news, indicating Willis had not progressed to the point of trying to build anything.

It took him almost an hour to download all the recordings of the five cameras he had installed on the property. Since the cameras were set to trigger by movement, the data was at least reduced but still plentiful. Only the one monitoring power contained a considerable amount of data because the dial on the meter was always spinning. As Albert looked through the rest of the images, he was surprised to see a small herd of elk move past. He had no idea elk would be so close to the Bay area. The rest was pretty mundane stuff, except by the house and garage. He could see all the activity that happened around the garage when the sheriff and deputies were crawling all over the place. It was a wonder they didn't discover his equipment. The recording for the next day included an unmarked police car and a detective scouring the area, walking around looking at reports on a clipboard and verifying things.

Albert was surprised to see a lone figure walk onto the property and go into the shop and come out minutes later. It was just getting light, so the pictures were not clear. The figure disappeared off the camera covering that area and headed for the house. It took Albert a few minutes to find the correct file for the camera at the rear of the house and watch as the intruder broke in through the back door. Interesting. Probably some neighbor who wanted to see what they could loot. The files showed the figure come out, but it was not light enough to see if he was carrying anything.

Other than a few deer coming up to the back porch eating Mrs. Willis's flowers, it showed nothing until a Dodge pickup drove up. The driver leaped out of the truck and took a circuitous route jumping from one thing to another and finally to the porch. He didn't seem to have anything either when he left and used the same path back to the truck leaping from the spot to spot. Except for one brief slip off a rock, the person made it to the vehicle where his partner waited. There was a mixed breed dog in the bed of the truck that Albert thought he had seen before. Maybe at Sam's Place.

Albert decided to wait until he was in a safer place to review the rest of the files. Now that things seemed to have calmed down in the area, he hoped to be able to check things more regularly. He took the fire roads to the main road and had no trouble with the gates because he'd overheard in Sam's Place that the CDF had access to all the properties to fight wildfires. These CDF locks used a standard key. He immediately asked his contacts to send a copy of the CDF key to him at the hotel. It worked nicely with his USGS cover. Albert always made sure to stop at several places along the road so the locals would get used to seeing the truck with the USGS markings.

CHAPTER 10 - FRIDAY LATE MORNING

Determined to use the time efficiently, Dan asked Wally to do the recording again. As they entered the shop, Dan quickly confirmed someone had disturbed things since the first time. Maybe his uncle was right and the detective had gone through the scene and moved things, but it didn't feel right to Dan. Looking at the toolbox, Dan was impressed by the custom machine work Willis or someone had done on the securing mechanism. There was a sudden metallic squeak that sounded muffled below the shop. A low growl rumbled in Syd's chest.

"Easy, Syd. It's probably a loose piece of tin siding on this old shop." They stood listening for a minute, then moved the toolbox out of the way and opened the panel. When they slid open the plywood and peered into the stairwell, the lights were on in the room below making the stairs easily visible.

Dan turned back to his uncle. "Looks like you forgot to turn the lights off down there."

"No way. Check the tape." Wally had carefully recorded everything to prove he left things as they should be.

"Well, they're on now." Dan's eyes got bigger as it hit him. He whispered, "Someone must be down there." Dan picked up a four-foot section of pipe used as a handle for the hydraulic floor jack. He also grabbed a mechanic's mirror from the top of the toolbox. "You stay here."

Wally started to protest until he saw the intense look Dan was giving him. Syd immediately sat down and waited for Dan's next command.

Dan eased down the stairs with the pipe at the ready, cursing every small squeak the wooden stairs made. When he reached the bottom step, he paused and listened, hearing nothing but the dog's panting above. The mechanic's mirror was a one-inch mirror on the end of an extendable handle. Dan extended it as far as it would go and used his left hand to hold the mirror out near the ceiling so it would be less likely to reflect light into the room. He could see no one. Moving the mirror around showed no attackers near the door. Once satisfied, he peeked around the corner. The room was empty. Dan stepped into the room and leaned to look down the row of bookshelves that were not visible from the door. No one. A red light was lit above the doorway. What the heck did it indicate? Were they in some danger? He had a sudden idea.

"Hey, Uncle, do me a favor and close the panel by you and open it again." Wally gave him a bewildered look but did as he asked. The light stayed on.

"Anything?" Wally asked when he popped his head back in the opening.

"No. Now go open and close the shop door." Again, his uncle did as he asked. The light remained on when he heard the door of the shop.

"How about now?" Wally was back at the opening.

"Nope. Is there any wire attached to the metal ring where the toolbox locks into the floor?" Dan heard his uncle moving around upstairs.

Wally stuck his head into the stairway. "Yes, one on each end."

"Okay, see those jumper cables on the pegboard beside where the toolbox goes?"

"Yeah."

"Run it from one to the other of the two with the wires." Dan waited. The red light went out. "Thanks, Uncle. I figured out the light by the door. You can come down now."

Wally started down the steps, only to be passed by Syd. Meanwhile, Dan took a cursory glance around the room. He needed to recheck the recording, but it looked as if some things were moved since Wally had been here. Most notably, the map that had been above the desk was gone. As soon as Syd sniffed around the area, she headed for the rear wall. With her paws on both sides of the hatch in the wall, she started growling. Dan turned to Wally.

"Did you replace the whiteboard when you left?" They stood looking at it sitting on the floor against the rear wall.

"I thought I did, but you can't see it on the tape from the door, so I'm not sure."

Dan moved cautiously to the rear wall. Syd looked at him, then at the wall, barking twice. With Wally behind him holding Syd's collar, Dan tried the handle for the hatch. It wouldn't budge. He inserted the pipe he was carrying to gain leverage and tried again. It was locked. He looked at his uncle.

"I think it's time for a strategic retreat," he whispered.

With that, they moved into the center of the room. Dan looked around for anything obvious he should take with him to protect from being stolen. He had no idea, so he took the camera and did a slow scan of the desktop and the room. He grabbed the recliner Willis used for his reading and started to move it toward the wall to block the hatch. As it moved, a hardbound lab book fell out from between the seat and the side of the chair. Dan picked it up and leafed through it. It was filled three-quarters of the way with Willis's scribbling and drawing. There were also some formulas and calculations in it.

Dan handed it to Wally. "Man, he was old school," he said, pointing at the drawings. "It makes no sense to me but could be significant."

Wally looked through it and shook his head. They went to the stairs and Dan turned off the lights. After exiting upstairs, Wally carefully slid the plywood back in place and closed the pegboard section. Dan rolled the toolbox in place and applied the locks. At the shop door, Dan held out his hand to stop his uncle from going through it.

"Let's see if he comes out," Dan whispered as he crept toward the toolbox. He still had the jack handle in his hand. Wally sat on an upside-down milk crate on the floor. Syd looked from one to the other curiously. They heard nothing downstairs. After twenty minutes of waiting, Dan headed toward the door. Once outside with the door closed again, he turned to his uncle. "Maybe there's another way out of there. We should move to where we can see the area behind the shop." Dan walked over to his truck and pulled a pistol from under the seat. He possessed a concealed weapon carry permit because there were occasionally pot growers who hid grows on parkland nearby. He generally kept it there for when he was out in the backcountry. Dan started to walk away from the truck, stopped and turned around again. He grabbed his iPad from the console and headed for the line of trees at the edge of the Willis property.

"What do you need that for out here? Gonna check your email?" Wally asked, grinning.

Dan looked at his uncle, saw Wally smiling, and realized his uncle had tricked him. Wally played much dumber about technology than he was. He enjoyed messing with Dan every once in a while and knew there was no way Dan could access the Internet out here even if the iPad had cell capability.

Dan shook his head. "No, I was gonna go online and order you a hearing aid." He laughed. "Actually, the battery is dying in the video recorder so I may need to use this and my phone." When he turned on the iPad to check the battery, it opened to the Wi-Fi settings page because Dan had been playing with the configuration page at his house.

Dan looked at his screen. "Holy crap, there's a network out here."

"Did Willis have one?" Wally edged over to look also.

"No, he didn't trust Wi-Fi. I asked him once when I was helping him and wanted to look something up." Dan paused, remembering.

"He hardwired his computers in his house so they would be more secure."

"This network is named VIDSURV. That's a weird name." He looked around. "Keep an eye on the shop for me, will ya."

Dan extended his arm in front of him and watched the screen, monitoring the strength of the Wi-Fi signal on his iPad. As he came into the view of one of the cameras, it activated, including a brief check of the network. The indicator on Dan's iPad surged, causing him to spin in the direction indicated by the screen. A few seconds later the signal faded.

"Damn, I had it. Where's that signal?" At this statement, Syd perked up and began circling Dan.

"I think Syd understood you." Wally was watching the dog.

Dan looked up from the screen, watched Syd's behavior and realized what was happening. "Find the cell phone, Syd. Find it, girl."

Syd began moving faster. She circled a few more times, sniffing, and finally put her paws up on the trunk of a tree. Dan and Wally ran over to her. She leaped at something just out of her reach. Dan could see a six-inch square box painted in a camouflage pattern. A strap wrapped around the branch. Dan looked more closely at the camera. There was a hole in one corner. He had seen similar units and even had one himself. Hunters used them to record wildlife activity in the woods. These were battery powered, motion activated and usually contained a hard drive or solid-state memory to store the files until the owner returned to retrieve them. Since this one sent out a Wi-Fi signal, it must be able to be accessed remotely for data retrieval. However, it did not appear to be the primary source of the network signal, so there must be a router somewhere near. That would indicate there was more than one camera.

Dan went to his truck and retrieved some bolt cutters from his toolbox. The straps on these cameras had thin steel cables in them for reinforcement. Using the bolt cutters, he cut through the band

and looked closer at the device. The camera was not a standard wildlife version you could buy at a hunting store. It was a custom setup, modified to add the Wi-Fi. He took it to the tailgate of his truck and used a hammer and large screwdriver to punch out the locking mechanism on the side of the cover so he could open it. Inside were a slot for a memory card and a port for connecting an Ethernet cable. He removed the battery and put the unit on the front seat of his truck. Grabbing his iPad again, he slid the tools into a backpack he had retrieved, threw it over his shoulder and turned to Syd.

"Find the phone." He motioned out toward the trees. Syd began circling and sniffing again. Now that Dan knew what to look for, he scanned the trees in the area as he walked, occasionally glancing at the signal indication. Within a few minutes, Syd was standing at the base of another tree, looking up and barking. Dan jogged over to the dog.

"Good girl. Good Syd." He gave Syd a pat on the shoulder. The dog responded with a high-pitched bark and leaped at the trunk of the tree. Dan climbed and retrieved the second camera unit using his bolt cutters.

"Find another one, girl. Go get it." Instead of circling, this time Syd shot off in a straight line, nose down, and ran a fair distance. He looked at Wally and said, "Look at her go."

"I don't want to burst your bubble or anything, but she's simply following the scent of the guy who planted them." He watched the dog running, nose down.

"I don't care how she does it," Dan said as he smiled, pleased with Syd's ability.

Syd began circling, occasionally looking to make sure Dan followed. She circled again with her nose to the ground and eventually sat at the base of a tree and barked once, glanced at Dan, then up at the tree. Dan could have sworn the dog was smiling.

When he viewed the display on his iPad, the Wi-Fi signal was showing full strength. In the tree, he could see a different-looking box about fifteen feet off the ground. Syd had found the router.

He gave Syd a pat on her shoulder. "Good job, girl," Dan said as he continued to pat her shoulder. Syd whined and put her paw on the trunk of the tree looking intently at the box.

Climbing the tree, Dan sat on a limb and examined the box. He opened it using his hammer and screwdriver, which took several blows. Once it was open, the box contained a consumer-grade Wi-Fi router attached to a small twelve-volt battery, likely from a motorcycle. Dan was familiar with this router because it was the same model he had at home and so he knew some of its vulnerabilities. Putting the tools in his backpack, he grabbed his iPad again.

Dan opened an app on his iPad called Network Toolbox. He hoped whoever placed the router left some of the default settings in place, which would make it much easier to break into it. First, Dan tried to ping the router using several common IP addresses, which checks to see if you can talk to another device on the network. On his second attempt, it responded. Now that he knew its IP address, he used it to try to connect through the Internet browser. A login screen came up. He tried a few commonly used passwords for the administrator login. Since he owned this same type of router himself, he knew the manufacturer added a login and password to the box so they could do troubleshooting. He tried their backdoor login consisting of 'system' and 'system' as the password. He was in. Apparently, the person who set this router up was either in a hurry or assumed no one out in the sticks would be able to crack it.

Dan accessed the configuration web page. It listed all of the devices connected to it, so he was able to tell there should be three more cameras active because there were three IP addresses on the network. There was a network extender, basically another router, also active. The interface gave him the IP addresses of each. He quickly found the extender because it was always broadcasting on the network. However, it was some distance away from everything else. Dan assumed this was to make it easier for the owner to retrieve the data without having to come onto the property. Once he located the extender, Dan returned to the primary router and began his search for the cameras.

One by one, he pinged the cameras, making them wake up and start responding. As soon as each did, he told Syd to find them. Within ten minutes all three were located. One was at the rear of the workshop and house with a view of the road leading into the property. The second was at the front of the house. The third one didn't make any sense to Dan. It pointed at the electric meter for the property. He wondered why someone would monitor Willis's electricity usage. As he walked to his truck with the last one, he signaled to Wally, who had climbed on top of a water tank near the shop to keep watch for the intruder.

"Did you see anything?"

"Not a thing, except you running around climbing trees," Wally said, climbing down and walking toward him. "Should we wait him out?"

"No. I don't think we need to since we probably have a video of whoever entered the shop." He motioned toward the pile of cameras on the seat of his truck. "Let's take this back and look at it to see what we can learn."

"Don't you think we should turn those over to the sheriff?" Wally asked, giving him a look of concern.

"Hey, they could be Willis's security system for all we know. It won't hurt to check them out." Dan realized Sanchez would probably not be pleased he removed them. He got caught up in the heat of the hunt. Now they even had his fingerprints all over them.

"Is that the story you're going with?" Skepticism replaced concern.

"That's my story and I'm sticking with it," Dan said, wishing he felt as confident as he sounded. "Look, Uncle, you're the one who broke into the crime scene and found a secret room. We're in pretty deep here when we finally talk to the sheriff."

Wally stared at the ground and rubbed the back of his neck. It was a habit when he was thinking or nervous. "Ah hell, in for a penny, in for a pound, I guess. Let's go see what's on these."

As he walked back to his truck, Dan took stock of what they had with them. "Hey, where's the notebook?" Wally looked around and wrinkled his forehead in thought.

"I think I set it on the workbench when we were replacing the toolbox," Wally said grinning sheepishly. "I'll go grab it and meet you at your place."

"Okay, but poke your head in to make sure it's clear before I head out," Dan said and pulled his truck up near the front of the shop. Wally slid the door back and turned on the light. He bent and looked under the Jeep that was on the lift about four feet off the ground. It was left raised after removing Willis's body. The notebook was on the bench a few feet inside the door. Seeing nothing, he waved to Dan, who started down the dirt road away from the property.

Wally went into the shop and grabbed the notebook from the workbench. He turned and walked back out, turning off the lights and closing the door as he did. Wally could see the dust from Dan's pickup off in the distance. The notebook was in his left hand as he reached for the door handle of his truck. Before he touched it, someone struck him from behind. His right arm went up instinctively to protect himself, then everything went black.

~ ~ ~ ~

"Shit!" Albert exclaimed as he threw the television remote across the room. He had been reviewing the files downloaded from the cameras while in his hotel room, half watching the local news. He had already been concerned the level of activity around the Willis place would lead to the discovery of his cameras now that the sheriff's office was crawling all over the property. He decided he would return to remove some of the equipment tomorrow. But even if they were discovered they could not be traced to him. That was when this second surprise hit him like a jolt from a stun gun.

Sitting on the edge of the bed, he was dumbfounded when an image popped up, pulling his attention away from a news story. There on the screen of his laptop was his own picture as he placed one of the cameras. Unaware it was turned on, his movement strapping it on the tree had tripped it to record. —there was a full facial shot of him right in front of the lens.

"God damn it!"

He was furious. He shot out of the hotel room, almost forgetting the keys to his Jeep. It was time to get those cameras out of there, now. During the long drive back to the site, he remembered something else that did not improve his mood. He was in such a hurry earlier when downloading the files that he forgot to delete them from the cameras. He tried to settle himself down when he came around a tight turn on the one-lane road and almost hit a large propane truck coming the other way around the corner. After a stressful forty-five minute drive, he arrived at the property. Albert immediately knew something was seriously wrong when he could receive no signal from his Wi-Fi network. Perhaps the router's battery had died.

He found a place to hide his SUV and began the hike to retrieve the equipment, though he was nervous about traipsing around at this time of the day. After frantically searching for almost an hour, he came to the realization his equipment was gone. Sitting back in his rented Jeep, his anger turned to panic.

What the hell else can go wrong? He rested his head against the steering wheel. He sat rocking in the front seat, trying not to hyperventilate. Whoever had those cameras could definitely trace them back to him now. How embarrassing it would be to blow his cover. He must get that equipment back.

Michael L. Patton

CHAPTER 11 - FRIDAY AFTERNOON

When Dan arrived at his place, he saw Ed's truck heading the other direction coming from the barn beyond his small house. The barn at Hawk's Nest was not as large as the one on the Rockin' A since it only needed to store hay for the local cattle. He pulled up alongside so the drivers' doors facing each other.

"I was just checking on you. I hadn't seen you or Wally at the shop for a while. With everything going on around here lately, I didn't want to let it go too long." Ed's smile revealed both relief and tension.

"We're fine. We were checking up on the Willis property. I found a bunch of wildlife cameras all over the place." Dan patted the pile on the seat beside him. "You don't know if Willis set them up for security do you?"

"He never mentioned anything like that," Ed replied. He thought for a second. "Why would anyone else set them up, unless maybe Thronson did?"

"I don't think so. These were all configured together on a Wi-Fi network." He held one up and pointed to the Wi-Fi card. "I think these were custom made. When's the last time you saw the county with anything this hi-tech?"

"Maybe they got some stuff from Homeland," Ed said as he shrugged.

"Well, I'm at least gonna look at it to see if I can find anything. You're welcome to come. I got some other things to tell you too," Dan said as he put the camera back on the seat. Dan continued to the house, waiting there as Ed turned around and pulled up behind him.

They went into the house and each grabbed an iced tea from the refrigerator. Dan sat at his computer and pulled the cards out and uploaded the files to his hard drive. He went to the couch, picked up the remote, and directed his smart TV to access the information on his computer. "We'll have a better picture using the big screen."

Ed looked at the TV then the computer and asked, "When did you get this fancy setup?" He was not averse to technology, but at his age it seemed to be accelerating a little faster than he could keep up.

"I have better luck streaming movies through my computer, so I bought the smart TV last year. I hardly ever watch regular TV anymore, or even satellite." Dan spent more time watching videos on YouTube about machining techniques than he did watching movies.

The files contained date and timestamps associated with them, so he picked one of the earliest ones. It showed a few animals wandering around the property, mostly deer and rabbits. Suddenly a picture showed bright morning sunlight. They could see a truck coming into view.

"Hey, that's my truck," Ed exclaimed as he pointed at the screen.

"Yeah, this is the morning we found Willis if the timestamps are right."

"Maybe we'll see who did it." Ed frowned. "But that would be pretty stupid to record yourself committing a murder."

"Dumber things have happened," Dan responded but didn't take his eyes off the screen. "It sure wasn't in this camera file, but maybe one of the other ones caught something."

On the recording, the truck disappeared behind the shop. The screen jumped to the time when the next movement triggered it to record. Two sheriff's cars arrived. Dan sped through the recording showing the deputies searching the area around the shop and putting up crime scene tape.

"There are five cameras," Dan said as he checked the timestamps on the files again. "That camera was activated first. The others all have times starting slightly later."

While viewing the information from the fourth camera, they hit pay dirt. "Holy shit," both said in unison. There on the screen was a shot of the face of the man installing the camera.

Ed nodded at the screen. "That's definitely not Willis."

"It's not Thronson or Spinelli either," Dan added as he picked up his phone and took a picture of the TV screen. He saw Ed staring at him. "Trust me. It's easier than trying to print an image from a video. Plus I have it saved on my phone now."

"The first person you're gonna show is Thronson," Ed said as he walked over toward the phone.

Dan did not even seem to hear him. "Man, he looks vaguely familiar," Dan said, mostly to himself as he stared at the screen. "Papi, does…" He looked around the room and his eyes grew wide with excitement. "Hey, where's Wally? With all these distractions, I forgot. He should have been here by now."

Dan stood up and headed for the door.

"I'm calling the sheriff," Ed said firmly, putting his hand on Dan's arm as he walked past. "Maybe you should wait."

"It'll take them an hour to get here. I'm not waiting for anybody," Dan said, not looking back. He kept walking and headed out the door. "You do what you gotta do."

He went to his truck and only paused long enough to ensure his pistol was under the seat and loaded. Ed watched the Dodge disappear in a cloud of dust as he heard the sheriff's office phone ring. When Ed stayed in the house on the phone, Syd remained on her bed in the corner. It was not until she heard Dan's truck start that she stood up and looked out the window. When Ed opened the door to leave she immediately bolted out and across the fields in pursuit of Dan's truck. Concerned with locking up, Ed did not even notice her exit the house.

~ ~ ~ ~

Wally woke up in the dark. It was cool and slightly damp. His hands and feet were bound. Lying prone on the ground, he was gagged and could feel a blindfold around his head. Maybe it was a floor. It smelled musty. He tried to roll over and sit up. It wasn't easy to do, and he ended up sitting on his hands because a rope went from his wrists down the back of his legs to his ankles. After a few minutes, he needed to move to his side to get circulation back into his hands.

Turning his head to listen, he could barely hear his own feet scraping on the floor. His ears felt funny, and he finally realized his captor went through the trouble of putting earplugs in his ears. Somehow that made him feel violated. He lay there thinking for a few minutes. *If he didn't want me to hear things, it must mean I am near other people or might be able to tell when he comes and goes.*

Wally tried to rub the side of his head against the ground to loosen the earplugs. The gag in his mouth also covered his ears, causing the rubbing to have no effect on the earplugs. It did, however, loosen the blindfold a bit. He kept working at it until he managed to scrape the blindfold from his eyes, which did not help because it was pitch-dark. A wave of fear spread over him thinking of how vulnerable he was. He tried to calm his breath and regain control.

He swung his legs in an arc to see if there was anything near him, but being hog-tied he could not move very much. A few feet behind him was a hard surface like a wall. He couldn't touch anything in front of him. There was no way to swing his legs upward to check the height of the ceiling above him. Scooting back, he moved until he could touch the wall. He felt around as much as he could, hoping to find something sharp or pointed he could use on the ropes. He screamed in frustration when he came up empty but could barely hear his cries for help.

Jerking while trying to kick the wall, he banged his head, causing him to remember the blow from behind. He saw stars and felt sick to his stomach.

Oh God, don't let me puke with a gag in my mouth. He tried to remain calm and breathe slowly again by telling himself he was at home in his bed. Waves of fear swept over him, followed by short stints of composure. Gradually the panic subsided. Finally, as the feelings of nausea passed, he mercifully passed out.

☐

~ ~ ~ ~

Spinelli was on a routine patrol near the edge of the hills when the call came in. He had been intentionally avoiding the area since the last encounter. The sergeant tried to talk him into taking a few days off after being locked in a trunk overnight, but with all the kidding he got at the station he was not going to give the other deputies another reason to harass him. Spinelli mainly avoided the hills after the sergeant warned him about causing any more hard feelings with the locals. He didn't understand why they would be upset with him, as he seemed to end up on the short end of most of the encounters.

Once they began sharing information, he had at least come to some level of understanding with Dan. Spinelli didn't mind him telling the stories at the station because Dan did not make him sound like an idiot, but rather a victim of circumstance. He seemed to be okay, but Spinelli did not want to tangle with his uncle, Ed. Messing with that old guy was like poking a grizzly.

The radio said one of the locals called with some urgent

information regarding the Willis case, and also concern that someone may be missing. *Maybe they're finally starting to realize the sheriff's department is here to help and will start cooperating,* he thought. He wondered what the information could be and hoped this was not a wasted trip because someone's dog found an old shoe somewhere.

He drove the road at a moderate pace, his flashers on so the locals would know he was on a call. He was not interested in really pushing it because he didn't want to be the first on the scene if he didn't have to be. The radio said to meet the caller at the Willis property. Spinelli was not sure who the caller was but was not particularly happy someone was once again traipsing around at the murder scene. It did bother him when Thronson did not back him on insisting the locals stay off of the property. If it was still an active investigation, he assumed the lieutenant would be more concerned about the integrity of the scene. Spinelli would do what he could, but it was really in the hands of the detective. His new mantra was to do his job well and let others take care of theirs.

~ ~ ~ ~

Dan did not see Wally's truck on the road from Hawk's Nest. As he passed the Rockin' A, he looked down at the property to see if Wally stopped at the shop. There was no sign of him. When he turned onto the road to the Willis property, he strained to see if the little Toyota was around. To his disappointment, the truck was not where it was when he left. Could his uncle have misunderstood where they were going? He knew Wally would not go home before viewing what was on those cameras because Wally was as curious as Dan.

Dan wished he had reviewed all of the files. He shook his head. There was no way he could stay there looking at video wondering about his uncle.

Damn it! Why can't we get better cell reception up here? Dan knew the logical answer, but there were times when it would make things easier. Of course, there were times Dan was happy to be unreachable. You take the good with the bad. Since he was at the Willis place, he thought about possibly using the landline in the house. However, looking at the time on the dash clock it showed Wally did not have quite enough time to get home yet. *Maybe I'll try in a little while. First, a look around again.*

Stepping out of the truck, Dan could see dust from a vehicle coming down the road. He stood up on the side step of his Dodge to get a better look, hoping Wally saw him and turned around. It was Ed.

"Sheriff's on the way," Ed said as he climbed out of his truck and walked up to Dan. "You need to slow down a bit. We don't even know if Wally went home, or went off to do something."

"You're right," Dan admitted, but Ed could tell he wasn't buying it. "So I guess you didn't pass him along the way either?"

"No. Did you stop by the Rockin' A? Maybe he stopped there. I was in such a hurry to catch up with you I didn't slow down to look."

Dan shook his head. "Yeah, I looked, but his truck wasn't at the shop or the house." He wrinkled his brow as he thought of something. "Why were you in such a hurry if you don't think anything's wrong?"

"I know you're worked up, so I don't want you charging in there and getting into trouble with the sheriff." Ed swept his arm toward the barn and the house. "I wanted to make sure you stayed outside the shop. Especially since Thronson should be here anytime." He gave Dan a serious look. "I don't know if you realize this, but you can be a bit bullheaded occasionally," Ed said with a smile.

"Says the pot to the kettle."

Dan did not tell Ed about the room they found. He almost had when they were watching the video files but it would have set Ed off, and Dan would have gotten another talking-to. Still, he felt guilty about not sharing and wondered how, and if, it would be possible to tell Thronson. His thoughts were interrupted by a car coming up the dirt road. They both turned to see a sheriff's car. It was Deputy Spinelli. Rather than the sense of dread he previously felt, a smile spread across Dan's face.

"Hey, Spinelli." Dan stuck out his hand to shake.

Ed looked a bit taken aback.

"Dan," Spinelli responded. He nodded toward Ed. "Mr. Wyath."

"Deputy." Ed didn't offer his hand.

Spinelli stood awkwardly for a few seconds. "You spend more time over here than at your place, don't ya?" Spinelli looked at Dan. After a tense second, he winked and laughed. "So what's going on? I heard you have some new information and someone may have disappeared."

"We've had a few developments," Ed volunteered. "Should we get into it now, or wait until the sheriff shows up?"

"Well, sir, he's not the actual sheriff. He's my lieutenant," Spinelli corrected Ed.

"I know. I know. But Thronson is the sheriff's office as far as I'm concerned," the older man responded a bit too emphatically. Ed was not fond of being corrected. "I don't want to have to repeat myself a dozen times."

"Can you tell me, in general, what's going on, sir?" Spinelli was trying not to set Ed off again.

Dan started. "We found some cameras on the property. I think they may have a picture of the killer on them." Dan glanced at Ed, trying to give highlights without going into detail. "We headed to my place to review them, at least we were supposed to, and my uncle never showed up."

"Is this your Uncle Wallace?" Spinelli looked at Dan and Ed. "So all three of you were here on the property?"

"No," Ed insisted. "I ran into Dan at his place."

Spinelli physically cringed at Ed's tone of voice. Fortunately, at that moment Thronson's SUV came into sight. A wave of relief swept over Spinelli. The three of them turned and waited.

Thronson pulled up and nodded to the three men standing near the shop. He climbed out of the SUV, putting on his hat. "I hear we've got some new developments. What did you guys find?" He looked directly at Dan.

Ed answered first. "We were just explaining to Spinelli here that Dan and Wally found some cameras scattered across the property. One of them has a picture of the guy who set them up, and it seems likely he's the killer." He stepped forward to shake Thronson's hand. Spinelli gave him a strange look.

"Well, that is interesting. What made you go poking around the property again?" Thronson asked, looking at Dan again.

"We decided to drive through the back way to our shop to check on the property, and we saw the door of Willis's shop was open slightly," Dan lied. He thought he was doing pretty well for making things up on the spot. "We suspected we might have the guy trapped inside, so Wally climbed up on the water tank to watch the area while I went around back." He thought a sprinkling of truth might help in case they found prints on anything. "My dog was with me and found the first camera."

"Where is the wonder dog?" Spinelli joked as he looked around.

It was the first time Dan realized Syd wasn't with him. He left in such a hurry she hadn't make it in his truck. He looked at Ed. "Did Syd come with you?"

"No. I haven't seen Syd." Ed looked around as if expecting the dog to pop out from one of the trucks.

"So, back to the camera," Thronson prodded.

Regaining his train of thought, Dan continued. "Um, I had my iPad with me and could tell the camera was sending out a Wi-Fi signal, so I started looking for others."

"Because it had Wi-Fi?" Thronson looked confused.

"Yes. Usually, these type of cameras, at least the ones sold in retail stores, operate as stand-alone. A deer hunter might put them out in the woods by his tree stand to see what kind of game is in the area."

"A deer hunter?"

"Well, or anyone wanting to capture pictures out in a remote area." Dan could see it didn't register yet. "I put them out to get pictures of some wild pigs that were tearing up the garden down by my place. I wasn't sure what kept eating my tomato plants."

Thronson nodded, beginning to catch on.

"They sell these cameras at hunting stores. They run on battery, are motion triggered, and they save the pictures to memory cards. They're meant to be out in the middle of nowhere, strapped to a tree." Dan went to his truck and grabbed one of the units and handed it to Thronson.

Thronson turned the camouflaged box over in his hand. "Oh. Now I get it."

"Look." Dan pointed to the small card that was plugged into the USB port. "Someone added this. They don't generally come that way, but someone wanted to network these to access them remotely."

"Okay. You lost me again. Because it's on a network means there is more than one?"

"Well, not exactly." Dan paused, trying to think of another approach to explain it. "I knew Willis pretty well. He didn't have a wireless network around here because he thought they are inherently insecure. If you have a Wi-Fi network, you must have a router that handles the signal, right?"

Thronson nodded, but Dan wasn't sure he was following.

"If you're going to go through the trouble to set up a network, why would you do it for only one?" Dan asked rhetorically. "You wouldn't. You would simply walk over and take the card out of the one. But if you wanted to install multiple cameras…" He paused to see if anything was sinking in.

"Ah. Then you could collect all the data from one place." Thronson's eyes lit up.

"Right," Dan acknowledged. "So I started looking for a router and other cameras. My dog, Syd, has learned to find my cell phone for me. Now I don't know if she was following the guy's scent or can hear the wireless signal somehow, but she managed to find all five cameras and two routers."

"Two routers?"

"Yes, there was a second one way over on the edge of the property," Dan said as he pointed. "I think it was added so he didn't have to come onto the property to download the files."

Spinelli nodded. "Makes sense."

"So you took all these?" Thronson looked at the pile of equipment.

"Yes."

"Instead of leaving them where they were?"

"I wanted to see what was on them." Dan didn't like where this was heading.

"You disturbed evidence, Mr. Williams." Thronson sounded testy.

"Well, Lieutenant, I was not sure who put them there," Dan said, backpedaling. "It could have been Willis to use as a security system."

"Number one, you were on property that was a recent crime scene." Thronson held up his hand counting off on his fingers. "Two, you acknowledged Willis didn't trust Wi-Fi. Three, you still haven't been completely cleared of involvement in the murder." He looked Dan in the eye. "Do you understand the seriousness of interfering with a murder investigation, Mr. Williams?"

"Yes, sir."

"The next ride you get into town will be for a much longer visit. Are we clear, Mr. Williams?"

"Crystal clear, sir." Dan knew he would be locked up if he mentioned the secret room.

"Lieutenant, there's still the issue of Wally missing." Ed jumped in trying to change the subject. "He was supposed to meet Dan at his house but we can't find him."

"We'll get to that in a minute, Ed." Thronson turned back to Dan. "So you took the cameras and what did you find?"

"I didn't go through all of them, sir. I was trying to do it chronologically because I thought it might show the time of the murder."

"And did it?" Thronson was losing patience.

"I didn't get that far." Dan realized he was completely flustered and probably not making sense. He must regain control. Thronson started to speak again, but Dan interrupted him. "What I did find was a picture of the person who installed the cameras and who could be the killer." He paused to take a breath and collect his thoughts. "His face was two feet from the camera." He reached into his pocket for his cell phone. "Here."

Dan showed Thronson the photo on his phone from the video. Spinelli was trying to see it but was much shorter than the two of them and did not get a clear view.

"Do you know this man?" Thronson looked at Dan and Ed.

Ed shook his head, but Dan stared at the picture on the phone again and said, "I feel like I may have seen him before, but I can't place him."

Spinelli finally reached up and grabbed Thronson's wrist and lowered the phone so he could see. "Hey, that's the USGS guy."

Everyone turned to him.

"I talked to him when he came in for lunch at Sam's Place the other day. They're doing some readings out here verifying some fault line or something." He was still getting blank stares from the others. "He drives a white Jeep Cherokee with USGS printed on the side."

Ed finally spoke up. "Yes, I've seen the vehicle."

"So have I." Dan looked at Spinelli. "Remember I told you I saw a light-colored SUV from that ridge over there the other morning when I discovered someone broke into Willis's house?" Dan gestured as he spoke.

"You think it was him?" Spinelli nodded toward the phone.

"He could have been checking on his cameras."

Thronson wasn't convinced yet. "Wait. Could the cameras have something to do with the USGS study? Maybe they include cameras for some reason. Maybe to record the ground shaking in an earthquake or something."

"Not likely," Ed jumped in. "Even if they did, the primary tool of the USGS is a seismograph. I found one back in the 1990s, after the Loma Prieta quake. They had placed it up on our property. It was about the size of a suitcase and you could see it was recording waveforms. They might use a camera, but it would be near a seismograph. These are clearly just cameras."

"Good point." Thronson started moving toward his vehicle.

One of the reasons Ed liked Thronson was that he stayed calm until all the information was gathered, but once it was he was a man of action. Thronson walked over to his SUV and tried the radio. The signal was weak, but still able to raise the dispatcher. Thronson informed them regarding what he learned and asked them to issue a BOLO, or be on the lookout, for the white Cherokee and gave a description of the driver. He remembered Wally was missing and instructed them to be cautious, as it may be a hostage situation. He requested that Detective Sanchez report to the crime scene if possible.

Walking back to the group, he asked, "Is this everything you collected?" Thronson pointed to the cameras and routers Dan stacked on his tailgate for Spinelli.

"Yes. But maybe we should take a better look around." He was hoping he could 'accidentally' lead them to the hidden room.

"You, my friend, are to come nowhere near this property again. Do you hear me?" He pointed his finger near Dan's chest.

Having someone poke him in the chest was something that would set Dan off. He had a drill instructor in the Marine Corps who had a bad habit of doing it. Dan broke the instructor's arm in a bar the night after he graduated boot camp. Surprisingly he did not press charges, so Dan went the rest of his hitch in the Corps with a clean record. Of course, he also earned a legendary reputation with his fellow Marines.

"Yes, sir." Dan knew he must comply. "Like I said, I have not gone completely through these files. You may find more evidence. As soon as I realized my uncle was missing, I came back here."

As he said it, Dan wondered what would happen when the tape showed him and Wally going into the shop several times. He would probably face charges, but at least he never went in alone. He was glad he took Chucky the first time.

"Do you need anything else from me, Lieutenant? If not, I want to go look for my uncle and my dog."

"No. Not right now." He pointed his finger again, but this time he was farther away. "Remember what I said."

"Yes, sir." Dan turned toward his truck. To his surprise, Spinelli came up to the door.

"Hey, Dan. Don't worry, I will keep you up to date on what we find." He patted Dan on the forearm resting on the window frame of the door. "And thanks for this stuff. It's the break we've been needing."

"Thanks, man." Dan reached to start his truck but Ed now appeared at the window.

"Hey, I've got to run into town. I'll look for Wally on the way and call you later." Ed gave his arm a reassuring squeeze.

"Okay. I'll either be at home or the shop." Just as Dan started the truck, someone came up to the window again. What now? He turned to see Thronson.

"Hey, Dan. Sorry I lost my temper. It could be my ass if we screw this investigation up." Thronson was once again his easy-going self. "Could you come and show me how to run these damned cameras?"

Dan laughed. "Oh, so now you need me." He shut off the truck and opened the door, acting as if he was going to hit Thronson with it. "Sure. Damned dumb county employees."

For the next forty-five minutes, they went through the files together.

~ ~ ~ ~

Wally came to with his head throbbing. He thought he could hear the sound of a truck motor, but it seemed far away. A surge of hope went through him. Struggling against the rope, he tried to kick the wall and yelled as loud as he could. Wally kept banging and screaming but didn't know how much noise he was making. The sound of the motor began to fade until it was gone. His hope was replaced by frustration as it grew fainter, causing him to continue flailing in a desperate attempt to free himself. Exhausted after several minutes of full exertion, he collapsed and passed out again.

CHAPTER 12 - FRIDAY EVENING

Detective Sanchez received the radio call from the dispatcher that Thronson wanted him to come to the Willis crime scene as soon as possible. He responded to the call, but because of the reception in the hills, Thronson could not hear him. Being on the east side of San Jose for another case, Sanchez decided to go immediately. Sanchez wished he could coordinate with whoever was up there so he had some idea what was going on and could give instructions to contain the scene, including posting a deputy if needed.

He heard the BOLO about the white Jeep, but only half listened to it since the patrol guys focused on traffic stops. What did grab his attention was when they mentioned there could be a hostage involved. He requested for the dispatcher to repeat the information and noted the vehicle type and color. It probably wouldn't matter— there were two other routes out of the hills, and because this one going to San Jose was the longest, it was the least likely to be used by the subject.

Trying to relax and enjoy the drive in the country, he used the time to review what little they had about this case. There was no clue for the motive, as the victim did not seem to have any enemies. He was older and retired, so love affairs and business partners were probably not a factor. The only suspect they had, Williams, was cleared for the most part. Sanchez's gut told him the guy was innocent. Whatever the new information was, it sure had Thronson excited. That didn't happen often.

The car came to a straight stretch, giving Sanchez a pretty good view of the west slope of Mt. Hamilton. He was at the top of the foothills and could see the road as it switch-backed up the side of the steeper summit. Sanchez thought he caught a glimpse of a white car.

He couldn't tell if it was an SUV. He slowed a bit and kept his eyes ahead to get a better look when the vehicle reached the next exposed section. It could be an SUV or a station wagon. Finally, on the fourth sighting, he could tell it was a white Jeep.

Sanchez radioed in the possible sighting and requested some backup to start up the hill. He found a narrow spot in the road that could be easily blocked by his unmarked car and set up a makeshift roadblock.

As the Jeep came around the corner, he could see the USGS marking on the side positively identifying the suspect vehicle. He pulled across the road, ensuring the passenger side of his cruiser was uphill and stepped out. Sanchez drew his service weapon and rested his hands on the roof of his unmarked car, gun aimed. The driver came to a stop about thirty feet away, shook his head and raised his hands up off the steering wheel. Once Sanchez handcuffed him and patted him down, he put his new detainee in the rear seat of the police car. Sanchez checked the vehicle for any signs of a hostage. Finding nothing, Sanchez moved the Jeep and his cruiser to a wide spot far enough off the road so traffic could get by. He would wait for a patrol car to come babysit the Jeep until they could get it to the police garage for the crime scene unit.

While sitting there Sanchez noticed a ranch truck coming down out of the hills. You could tell the ranch trucks by the flatbed that they put on the back of them. The driver pulled up beside them and he could see the passenger window of the pickup roll down. Sanchez rolled his window down in response.

"Everything okay? You need any help?" It was a man he recognized as Ed Wyath.

"Everything is under control. Thank you," Sanchez responded. He could see the rancher glance back at Stevens. Wyath waved, and slowly pulled away.

It was an uncomfortable position for Sanchez since he was not sure what information they discovered on the hill and did not know what line of questioning to follow. So they sat in Sanchez's car waiting.

"What am I being arrested for?"

"At this point, I was only told to detain you."

"Then why pull a gun on me?"

"My instructions were to proceed with caution, so I did."

"Look, I'm an agent for the Department of Energy. You can call my superiors if you want. I was on my way down to your headquarters to explain the surveillance equipment. Check my ID." The subject was getting irritated.

Since the suspect had his hands handcuffed behind him, Sanchez reached back, grabbed him by the shirt to keep control of him and took a wallet out of the inside breast pocket of his jacket. Sure enough, there was a DOE identification card in his pocket. The name on it was Albert Stevens.

Sanchez had heard nothing about surveillance equipment but decided to play it close to the vest. "I'm sure we'll get it all straightened out downtown, but right now we have to follow procedures, and that's what we're gonna do. A DOE badge does not give you a free pass on a suspected murder charge."

After a few minutes of silence, Stevens spoke again. "I work for the federal government. I was working a case. I doubt you have the security clearance for me to brief you, but you need to let me go."

"Well, we'll find someone with the right clearance that you can spill your guts to. But right now you're going downtown."

Sanchez remained quiet, hoping the awkward silence would make the suspect keep talking. Stevens, however, sat sullenly in the back seat throughout the wait and for the entire ride into town. Once they were at headquarters on West Younger Avenue, the suspect started raising holy hell until he quickly went through a captain, an assistant sheriff and the undersheriff ranting about security clearances. They confirmed Albert Stevens did indeed work for the Department of Energy, but that alone impressed none of the personnel who were dealing with his arrogant attitude.

He sat fuming in an interview room for an hour and a half while an FBI agent with Top Secret clearance drove down from the field office in San Francisco. An hour after that, Sanchez was taking Stevens to get his Jeep out of the impound lot where it had been towed but was informed of nothing about what the FBI learned. He returned to headquarters to await Thronson.

~ ~ ~ ~

Lieutenant Thronson arrived at headquarters about a half an hour after Stevens was released. He sat dumbfounded as he was read the riot act by the undersheriff for all the heat he had taken because of Thronson arresting federal agents and interfering with a federal investigation. As much as his boss hated the Feds attitudes, he was instructed to return the confiscated equipment to said federal agent promptly. Promising to comply, he and Sanchez left their dressing down and headed into the conference room where a deputy was guarding the confiscated evidence Thronson had brought.

Once they were out of earshot of the captain, Thronson finally spoke. "Why can't those federal assholes give us a heads-up when they are working in our jurisdiction?"

Sanchez laughed. "You don't have the clearance to know what's going on in your area, Lieu. Agent Stevens would have to kill you if he told you."

"But why DOE? How do those guys pop up in the middle of a murder investigation in the hills?" Thronson relieved the deputy of guarding the boxes of equipment. He sat in a chair at the end of the conference table.

"I did a little digging while we were waiting for the FBI to get here. I couldn't help wondering that too." Sanchez walked up to a whiteboard and began writing. "When he told me he was DOE, I wondered what the connection was." He wrote down Albert Stevens and DOE on the whiteboard. "The case we are working involves a retired employee from Lawrence Livermore Labs, which is run by the DOE." He wrote down Norbert Willis and LLL. "This guy Willis was a fairly well-known scientist back in his day. But why would they send an agent to set up cameras to watch a retired employee?"

"Did you find any reasons?"

"I'm only guessing here, but Willis's area of expertise was nuclear physics. The only other reference I found about him on the Internet was an interest in World War II history. He was pulled in as an expert on the Nazi weapons programs back when Germany was trying to develop Wunderwaffe, or Wonder Weapons, like the V-1 and V-2 rockets they used near the end of the war. Apparently, they were close to having a nuclear bomb too. The history was a hobby for Willis, but he became quite an expert in the area." Sanchez wrote nuclear physics and WWII history on the board by Willis's name.

"I still don't see a connection." Thronson gestured toward the board.

"Well, the DOE is the agency that controls all things energy, environmental and nuclear in the US. I checked, and they have a counter-terrorism, counter-proliferation division." Seeing Thronson's still blank expression, he continued. "Maybe they think Willis was sharing secrets with someone. Like I said, I'm just guessing."

"Maybe." Thronson did not sound convinced as he stared at the board. "You don't think the DOE killed off Willis?"

"No. I never thought of that." Sanchez turned to the table with the boxes. "Do you suppose we're allowed to look at this stuff? I wouldn't mind looking through the video files. Do you think we have clearance to make copies?"

"Probably not." Thronson smiled. "But we don't have to because Williams already did when he was showing them to me." He held up a USB stick.

"Great. Why don't you get these back to Secret Agent Man Albert Stevens." Sanchez's voice dripped with sarcasm at the mention of Stevens. "I'll start going through what's in the backup files." He took the memory stick from Thronson. "Any particular order I should start with?"

"Not really. I didn't review all the files, but one monitors the power meter on the Willis property. Weird, huh?"

"Well maybe DOE has their retirees on a strict energy diet." Sanchez laughed at his own joke. Thronson groaned.

~ ~ ~ ~

Dan worried about his uncle after leaving Thronson at Willis's place. Wally should have definitely checked in by now. Dan drove the few miles to the Rockin' A then went to the main house to use the phone. He called his Aunt Bobbie to ask if Wally had returned home. He hadn't, but she promised to have him call when he did.

After talking with his aunt, he decided to go check Hawk's Nest in case Wally took the fire roads down for some reason and got stuck or sidetracked. Once there, he found neither his uncle nor Syd. Dan paced around the kitchen for a few minutes feeling trapped. Thronson was dead serious about him not returning to the Willis property so he couldn't go there looking for clues to where his uncle went. Wally's truck was gone from Willis's, which meant he probably left the property. Dan could kick himself for taking off instead of waiting for his uncle. He'd been too excited to get a better look at the recordings and was not thinking clearly.

Dan drove all around the Hawk's nest property calling for Syd and looking for any sign of his uncle. He took the fire roads back to the Rockin' A, in case either of them had gone that way. He checked Sam's place, and everywhere else he could think would be likely. After having no luck, he ended up back at the Rockin' A.

Unable to sit still, he decided to go to the shop. He could try to distract himself with some work because they were starting to get behind on some things with all the interruptions lately. He arrived at the shop as the sun was setting. The sky was glowing orange and red to the west. It was quiet, and everything seemed peaceful. Dan tried to take a few deep breaths to calm himself, but he wouldn't be able to relax until he found his uncle. The only noises were the horses, which were calling out because they knew it was feeding time and Ed had not returned. Dan went about the business of tending the animals, giving some hay and grain to the horses and feeding the barn cats. He loaded a few bales of hay onto his truck and drove out to the pasture, where the cattle stood waiting by the fence gate. Dan spread it out for them. Something about completing the ritual of feeding and caring for the animals helped calm him a little. He sat on the tailgate of his truck watching the sun go down as the cattle grazed on the hay. Even with everything that was going on, the beauty captured his attention.

"God, I love it up here," he said to no one but the cows. Feeling a little restored, he decided to head to the shop and get some things done while he waited for Ed to get home.

The noise of the grinder he used to clean up welds on a set of shelves made him unsure if he heard something outside. When he stopped grinding and listened, he heard a car door with a squeaky hinge opening. Dan doubted Wally would drive after dark, but it could mean Ed was home. He set the grinder down and walked over to the door. Dan could see in the light outside that it had started to drizzle. Looking at the driveway on the property toward the main

109

house, he saw no sign of Ed or his truck. Then it struck him that the only other option was his truck. As soon as he cleared the garage door, he could see someone going through his Dodge.

"Hey," he yelled.

The figure peeked over the dash, but instead of getting out and running slid into the driver's seat. They always left their keys in the vehicles on the ranch in case someone needed to move something. Nobody ever stole anything around here. The inconceivability of it made him hesitate long enough it gave the figure time to start the truck.

The Dodge was parked about twenty yards past the shop door, closer to the pasture than the driveway after he came back from feeding the cattle. As he took another step, the headlights came on making him unable to see who it was, or if there were multiple people in the truck. He ran out to the middle of the driveway, cutting off access to the road, and waved his arms. He heard the diesel accelerate and for a few seconds thought the person was going to drive right at him. As the truck neared, however, it veered left and accelerated hard straight up the hill toward the main road. There were a few small mounds toward the bottom of the hill and a sharp rise of about thirty feet up to a barbed wire fence lining the main road.

Dan leaped at the truck, catching one hand on the top of the pickup bed and one foot on the back bumper. He clung for dear life and looked at the cab.

"Stop!" Dan screamed, but it was lost in the roar of the diesel. He could only see one person in the truck. The person looked taller than him based on where his shoulders came on the seat back. As Dan swung his right arm to get a second hand on the bed, the truck hit the first small mound and it pitched him off the bumper landing flat on his back. With the wind knocked out of him, he could only helplessly watch as the truck continued up the hill. As Dan fought to get his breath, the Dodge slowed, reaching the steep part. The driver hadn't put it in four-wheel drive in his hurry to escape. As a result, the rear wheels began spinning and digging deep ruts into the side of the hill. Still unable to breathe, Dan watched as the big Dodge inched its way up the incline digging furiously with the rear wheels. The vehicle halted for a second. Dan could hear the distinctive click of the hubs locking on the front wheels as the driver stopped long enough to put the truck in four-wheel drive. The engine roared to life again and all four tires began digging in. It gained momentum, cresting the hill fast enough the diesel had no problem snapping the three strands of barbed wire. If the driver were two feet to the right, he would have hit a wooden fence post in his blind charge up the hill. Dan heard the tires chirp as the truck hit the blacktop. It made a left and accelerated down the road. He could do nothing but lie there until his breath finally returned.

Dan cursed at the sky and watched the drizzle falling on his face until he could finally roll to his side. Once he could stand, he stumbled to the shop.

"Shit," he panted, still struggling a bit for breath. Why would someone take his truck, and how did they get up there in the middle of nowhere? He would have given them a ride into town if they asked. Now he wanted to choke them. *Could it have been anything to do with Willis? Maybe it's the killer that the Sheriff was looking for?* Things weren't making sense.

"I need to catch this bastard," he said, trying to think of what other cars were available. He still had the spare ranch truck at Hawk's Nest from the previous day when Ed picked him up from the sheriff's headquarters. With both Ed gone and Margaret still visiting her sister for a few days, the only other truck was an older pickup that belonged to Margaret's brother and hadn't been used in years since his death. Dan ran to where the old Chevy was parked.

"C'mon, baby," Dan prayed under his breath as he turned the key. When it didn't even click, he knew the battery was dead, as he suspected it might be. He had no transportation other than a tractor whose battery was also always suspect. It would be tough to catch up with the truck thief on an old Ford farm tractor.

"Give me a damned break." He slumped over the steering wheel, so mad he had tears in his eyes.

Dan sprinted to the main ranch house to use the phone. By the time he reached the door, it was raining steadily and he was soaked. He walked into the bathroom, washed some of the mud off of his face and grabbed a towel as he moved to the phone to call the sheriff's department. Maybe they could catch the guy heading down the hill with his truck. When he placed the receiver to his ear, there was no dial tone. This occasionally happened when it rained, causing the lines to get wet. It was also possible someone wrecked and hit a telephone pole. With so few customers out in the country, the lines were vulnerable to problems.

"Why don't you just kill me now, damn it." He slammed the phone back in its cradle. With no other options, Dan returned to the shop to lose himself in some work until Ed came home.

~ ~ ~ ~

By the time Albert left the sheriff's headquarters, it was dinnertime and there was heavy traffic downtown. He asked around and got a recommendation for a good burrito shop. Albert drove to Santa Clara Street and ordered a burrito at a place called Nacho's, attempting to wait out the traffic. Carrying his box of equipment into a booth in the back, he fired them up and began downloading and reviewing the videos. While watching the recordings, Albert noted the removal of the file folders and binder by Wally and his nephew. After an hour and a half of reviewing, he needed to follow up on several things, including trying to identify the tall figure in the videos.

His first order of business was to pay a visit to the Williamses and get back what they took. He may as well do it tonight.

The sun was starting to set as he began his drive up Mt. Hamilton Road. Fortunately, it was behind him for most of the climb. There were a few switchbacks that still caused him to face into the glare, but the red light reflecting off the mountainside with a clear sky above made the drive spectacular. He stopped at a wide spot to watch the Santa Clara Valley light up in the distance. From his vantage point, he could see most of the bay up to San Francisco. He allowed himself only a few minutes of enjoyment before getting on the road and focusing on his mission ahead. He didn't know where Wally or his nephew lived but saw them working at a shop on a ranch people referred to as the Rockin' A. One of them probably lived there.

Albert reached the summit, near the observatory, and began the descent into the San Antonio Valley. It started to rain, and by the time he reached the lower level it was pouring. The drive had taken longer than he thought and it was getting late. There was little moonlight because of the cloud cover, so the driving was slow for someone not familiar with the road. It was almost ten o'clock by the time he reached an area he recognized as familiar a few miles south of the Willis property. As he crested a small hill, he could see ahead of him that a truck was pulling off the road down on the next straightaway.

Albert slowed, noticing three vehicles just off the road in the bushes. He could see a man rushing from a white Dodge pickup with its lights still on toward a tan Jeep similar to what Albert was driving. It was not a Cherokee, but one of the other models recently introduced when Fiat purchased Chrysler.

The figure opened the cab of the Dodge and seemed to be transferring a few things into it. The third vehicle was a gray Toyota pickup furthest from the road. As Albert neared he strained to get a better look. He recognized the Jeep and was sure he had seen it at least once before because he noticed a National rental sticker on the windshield when it reflected in his headlights. Albert decided to stop under the pretense of asking if the man needed any help. He pulled to the right and swung the Cherokee around, heading back down the road. When he got to the Dodge, he eased off the blacktop and started toward the vehicles.

He didn't see the man at first and was in the process of rolling down his window when a tall figure stepped out from behind the Jeep. As the man realized Albert was approaching him, he took a shooting stance, raising a pistol and firing at Albert's windshield.

His windshield shattered with spider web cracks blocking Albert's vision and he felt a searing pain in his shoulder. He immediately floored the vehicle and turned the steering to the right, hoping to drive through the brush ahead of him and make it back to the road. What he didn't know was that beyond the brush was a drop-off into a small ravine where water flowed down to the valley floor. His Jeep punched through the brush and plunged ten feet, wedging itself between some boulders below. The front of the vehicle crushed like a soda can and the airbag deployed. Albert was knocked unconscious by the box of camera equipment that flew over the seat, hitting him on the side of the head. The Jeep sputtered and stalled as the pulleys on the front of the engine were impacted by the grill and radiator.

The last thing he heard before passing out was the sound of the rain easing up on the roof of the Jeep.

~ ~ ~ ~

Things were rapidly falling apart for Paulo. His mission was clear. He was to follow Agent Stevens until he found Dr. Willis. Once he located Willis, he was going to wait for a chance to infiltrate his lab and recover as much of his grandfather Erik's research as he could, including any information the old man had on the location of the missing submarines.

From the beginning of the week, his luck was in the toilet. After successfully shadowing the secondary target, Stevens, Paulo found his objective. During his first attempt at infiltrating the property, he was surprised by Willis.

"Where's my God-damned notebook, you bastard," Willis said, swinging a body hammer wildly at Paulo.

Paulo considered it a case of self-defense when he blocked the blow and shoved Willis away from him. Willis hit his head on the side of the car lift and crumpled to the ground, the hammer falling into the spreading pool of blood. Paulo lowered the lift to do a quick search of the Jeep before Willis woke up, but just as the rail got close to him the old guy kicked and his head went under it. Paulo was behind one of the lift's pillars and did not see Willis move until it was too late. He almost got sick when he glanced down and saw the car lift crushing Willis. Paulo picked up the hammer, at first assuming people would think it was the murder weapon. Staggering back he dropped it into the trash bin as he leaned over trying not to throw up.

"Ay Dios Mio!" he cried as he stumbled out of the garage. He returned to his hotel room to reassess his assignment.

The old scientist had gotten his hands on the original secret Nazi documents that had tracked the gold shipments to Argentina as the war was ending. Most of it was shipped by submarine, and several had been sunk off the coast, never to be found because no one had the information about what was on each ship. Perhaps until now. Willis had started piecing together information as a result of tracking uranium shipments to Japan. The Japanese had paid for the uranium in gold. Martin Bormann, Hitler's private secretary, had started redirecting the treasure to Argentina near the end of 1943 as the tide of the war began to turn. Since the Americans had seized the records of the ship movements, his grandfather had no luck in searching for the lost gold off the coast. It became apparent this guy Willis knew something based on inquiries he had made of a few people in Argentina who claimed to be witnesses to subs being sunk during the war. Paulo was to find out what the old man knew.

Returning to the scene the second time, he was interrupted by that nosy deputy. Paulo subdued the deputy and left him in the trunk, assuming he would be found. He was not a violent man by nature. His luck improved a little when shadowing the grumpy old man in the Toyota. Paulo saw him remove material. After searching the shop and the house, he couldn't believe this guy found old man Willis's hiding place. Paulo went back the next morning, redoubled his efforts in the garage, and found the loose panel behind the toolbox. He was in the secret room when he heard a vehicle approaching.

He ran up the steps and replaced the toolbox and the pegboard just in time. As his luck would have it, Grumpy showed up with a younger guy and came down to the secret study. Paulo overheard the young guy yell, 'Hey Uncle,' as they were trying to figure out the lights. If Willis had not built the safe room and escape exit, Paulo would have been caught. As he hid in the small, dark room, the dog was scratching on the other side of the hatch door. His heart raced as the handle of the latch rattled, but fortunately, it did not open. He waited for a while after hearing them leave, emerged from his hiding place, and snuck quietly up the stairs. Paulo got the secret panel open, the toolbox moved and entered the garage. Inside, he watched as the younger guy worked with the dog to find several devices that looked like square boxes around the property. The younger guy left, but the older man headed toward the shop where Paulo hid.

He caught Grumpy and tried to convince him to give up the materials he stole. He attempted to question him in both English and Spanish with no luck. The old man's only response was, "Fuck you, Poncho.'

Paulo got so angry that he cursed him in both his grandfather's

German and his own Spanish before giving up entirely. The grumpy guy did not speak German and might have no idea what was in his possession. *Why would he even want to take the documents?* But Grumpy would not give them up. Paulo left him tied in the small space behind the hatch to soften him up for a while, as the Americans say. He planned to return later and convince him after letting him go hungry a day or so—Americans are basically spoiled and weak people.

Paulo searched the old man's Toyota but there were no files or binders. The nephew seemed to work out of his truck, so Paulo hoped he stored the stolen material in it. Paulo wanted to search the Dodge for the files. He was sure they were significant since they removed them after spending so much time in Willis's shop. At least Paulo had the map that was in the secret room.

He hiked to the ranch to move in quietly. However, when he was going through the white truck the nephew caught him. Paulo had no choice but to take the Dodge. Unfortunately, he did not find anything of use in it except a cordless grinder with a cutoff wheel and a handgun. Shortly after discovering the gun, his mission was almost blown when Agent Stevens came driving up the road. Once Stevens doubled back, Paulo knew his mission would be compromised if he were seen. He couldn't allow that. Paulo was within reach of the information that was needed, knowing where most of it was and who had it. Paulo knew the agent would be able to place him in the stolen vehicles, so in that split second he did what he needed to do. Now Paulo had to move quickly. He must find those stolen files and leave the area. Somehow the nephew was the key.

Paulo took the big Dodge to where he hid his rental car and stashed the Toyota belonging to the one he called Grumpy. With so many vehicles there, now it was impossible not to notice them from the road. He climbed into his rental car and eased onto the road but heard yet another vehicle slowly coming from the south. He pulled off onto a dirt road a quarter of a mile from where he left the two trucks. There was a gate with multiple locks on it. He used the cordless Dremel tool to cut them, then pulled the Jeep through the fence and hid it behind some bushes. He returned and replaced one of the locks so the gate appeared secure. Fortunately, the approaching driver was moving slowly. The noise of the vehicle indicated it was a diesel truck. It was getting close now and he could see headlights coming from the south.

Paulo rushed to his Jeep, shut it off and lay down across the seat so it looked empty. To his surprise, the vehicle stopped where he'd left the other two trucks. However, after a few minutes it started again and proceeded up the road. Paulo moved farther down the dirt road, where the Jeep could not be seen, and crawled into the back seat. He would start early tomorrow.

CHAPTER 13 - FRIDAY NIGHT

Ed was in a good mood, even though he was driving a dark winding road in the rain. They needed the water and hearing it on the roof of the cab was actually a welcome sound. He traveled most of the way listening to the radio, where the meteorologists were warning about the severity of the storm just beginning. They stopped short of calling it the storm of the century. Heavy rains had been predicted earlier this year, but somehow they all missed the San Antonio Valley, so Ed hoped they would get enough to fill his ponds to last through the summer. Tonight, however, it had finally delivered, and it seemed to grow in intensity as he got closer to home. He turned the radio off when it started raining steadily to enjoy the sound of it falling.

Thank God it waited until I was almost home to start really coming down.

As he turned a corner and headed down a straight stretch a few miles south of the Willis place, he saw something in the bushes at the side of the road reflecting in his headlights.

Looks like taillights. It wouldn't be the first time Ed found someone who slid off the road. He slowed down as his truck approached where he saw the reflection. To his surprise, it was Dan's Dodge pickup. Parked right beside it was Wally's Toyota.

What in the world are those two up to? Ed pulled off the road, grabbed a flashlight and jumped out of the truck. Looking around, he could find no one in or around either vehicle. On the ground nearby was another set of tire tracks. Perhaps they met someone here.

With the rain coming down quite hard now, Ed was not interested in sticking around. Climbing into his truck, he wiped water from his face and took his cap off to shake the water off of it. His rear tires spun in the wet clay backing out onto the road. Ed hoped no one was coming and kept the accelerator down so he would not lose momentum. When he felt the rear tires grip the pavement, he let up, shifted to drive and headed up the road. Perhaps it was going to be a big storm.

As he came upon the Rockin' A, he could see the light on in Dan's shop. Since the incident with the prowler, he was not going to take any chances. He turned off the motor and put it in neutral, letting the truck coast down the hill into the yard. The gravel made some noise, but with the rain coming down hard on the tin roof of the shop he hoped it would drown out the sound. Stopping about thirty feet from the shop door, he eased out of the cab as he grabbed the rifle always carried wedged against the dash. He chambered a round and checked the safety.

He heard noise from the milling machine inside and wondered what kind of person would break into a place to make something, causing him to think it might be Dan. He moved quickly while the noise continued, knowing the position of the machine would require the person's back be toward the entrance. Peeking around the door, Ed could see Dan working. He kept his body protected as he scanned the rest of the shop. Satisfied no one else was there, Ed finally stepped into the room.

Dan shut off the machine and turned to put the piece on the table behind him. When he caught sight of Ed, he jumped and his hand automatically went to a wrench close by that he used to change bits.

"I thought I taught you better than to bring a wrench to a gun fight." Ed laughed.

It took Dan a few seconds to recover, but he finally smiled too.

"You almost got yourself shot, after my scare out here the other day," Ed continued.

Dan set the wrench down and nodded toward the door. "I was gonna try to distract you while I went for that." Ed looked to his left and saw the rifle propped beside the door. "Guess I should have kept it closer. I didn't hear you pull in."

"I didn't want you to. I saw the shop light on so I cut the engine at the cattle guard." Ed ejected the clip and the cartridge from the chamber. He put the round back in the clip and set both down on the worktable in from of him.

"I'm glad you're home. Somebody stole my truck."

"Really? Tonight?"

"From right outside the shop. I tried to stop them and they tore off straight up the hill." Dan pointed through the open door at the hill, where deep ruts were partially visible in the light on the outside of the barn.

"Did you have to let him tear holes in the side of my hill too?"

"I had hold of the back of the truck until he hit that first berm there. Bucked me off like a bronco." He nodded at the small mound at the bottom of the hill.

"Well, how much would it be worth to you to get it back?" Ed asked.

Dan frowned at him, unsure what he was getting at.

"I happen to know where it is. It's right up the road by the Drop-Off." Ed used the name the locals called the spot where the road dips down to the valley floor.

"Really? Anyone around it?" Dan was hoping to exact some revenge.

"No, just Wally's truck? Has he shown up yet?"

"He hasn't, and it's interesting that the trucks are in the same place." Dan stared at the floor thinking.

"Did you feed the animals?'

"Yes."

"Well then let's go get your truck back." He grabbed the rifle and clip off the table and headed out. Dan picked up the other one, turned out the lights and closed the door.

On the way to Dan's truck, Ed told him more about what he saw when he checked it earlier. They agreed they still needed to be careful. He also informed Dan about seeing that the detective had arrested the guy in the USGS Jeep on the way into town. Like Dan, Ed wondered who would have taken his Dodge since the killer was in jail. The rain eased up to a steady sprinkle. When they got to the trucks, they approached carefully, covering each other as they moved. No one was around. Dan looked over his uncle's truck. There were no signs of any damage or a struggle. He found no blood or indication of what happened to Wally. He checked his own vehicle. Other than a few scratches from the barbed wire and mud from digging its way up the hill, his Dodge was undamaged.

"Did they take anything?"

Dan looked around but saw nothing missing. He was glad he moved the binder and hid it in the shop. "No—" he stopped in midsentence, turned and looked under the seat. "Shit! He's got my pistol."

~ ~ ~ ~

Wally slowly came into consciousness hearing the distant sound of a dog barking. *Syd?* His head pounded and he still felt nauseous. He squirmed against the restraints and finally managed to roll to his other side. It was little comfort but felt somewhat better to change his position. He had no idea how much time had passed, or even what day it was. The total lack of sensory input from the darkness and the earplugs made him focus on the hardness of the floor. He felt as if he could almost feel every fiber in the rope around his wrists. The starvation for input made him focus on any sensory stimulus. The coolness of what seemed to be concrete against the side his face. The musty smell of the room he was in.

He listened, focusing as hard as he could. *Yes, it was definitely a dog.* He tried to cry out but could not tell if he made much sound. It sounded thunderous in his own head, but he had no way of confirming actual transmission of sound. Then he heard it—the dog's bark became more frantic. *Was it responding to him?*

Wally was silent for a few minutes until the bark slowed to an occasional yip. He yelled again and tried to kick. The dog seemed to respond with frantic, high-pitched yelps. It still sounded far away. *Where was he? Why did the dog not come running?* Wally yelled and kicked until, exhausted, he once again passed out.

~ ~ ~ ~

Sanchez had taken the video files home so no one could see him reviewing them. He began looking through the video files in chronological order, much the same as Dan had. As he watched the first bit of tape, he wondered what national secrets were going to be revealed by a few deer walking around in the trees on the Willis property. *Those feds are unbelievable with their clearances and bullshit.*

He came to the file that clearly showed Agent Stevens' mug full frame in the camera. "Way to go, dipshit," Sanchez said to the screen.

He viewed a few more of the video files until he came to the one for early Wednesday morning. A tall figure walked in from the western part of the property. The man moved cautiously, making him look suspicious. He slipped into the shop and remained there for a good five minutes according to the timestamp, then reappeared and walked toward the Willis house. The view of the Willis home was blocked by the camera's angle, but Sanchez was sure this was when someone had broken in. After about fifteen minutes, the figure appeared on the other side of the building and walked around it. He came near but not close enough to get a good facial shot.

That guy is too tall to be Agent Stevens. The suspect suddenly looked upward and to the east. He trotted off toward the west and out of range. Sanchez noted the time.

In the next set of frames activated by the motion sensor, a truck came in from the east. It must have been what frightened off the tall figure. Sanchez was pretty sure it was Dan Williams' Dodge pickup. There were two people in the truck and a dog in the bed. It disappeared behind the shop, which would be the rear of the house. The Dodge was out of sight for three or four minutes, then appeared out from behind the building and left the property in more of a hurry than it arrived. He remembered that Williams said they checked on the property and found the back door open. When Sanchez noted the time again, he wasn't sure Dan knew how close he came to walking in on the guy.

Sanchez's chronological search took him to a different video file. This one showed the rear of the garage and the house. He caught a glimpse of the tall figure coming in from the west after leaving the shop, the entry of which was blocked from this angle. The suspect walked across the yard and went up on the back porch. No tools could be seen, so he must have used a credit card to break in. Sanchez stopped the video and checked his case file for pictures that showed the lock on the back door. It was a standard door handle with no deadbolt and would be easily compromised. The person disappeared into the house briefly and came back out. Sanchez noted the timestamp. The clocks of the two cameras were different by only nine seconds.

A sudden wave of exhaustion made Sanchez look at his watch. It was nine-thirty already. Should he keep going through these files, or start again in the morning?

His wife poked her head in the door of the study. "You working all night?"

"Just fifteen more minutes," he promised, but the next file changed the case in his eyes.

A few hours after Williams and his uncle patrolled the Willis property, his uncle returned. It showed him walking around the outside of the shop and going inside. He was inside for approximately twenty-five minutes, and when he emerged again, he carried what looked like a folder and a binder. *Why in the world did he enter the garage? More importantly, why did he remove evidence from the crime scene?* Good old Uncle Wally just jumped to the top of the suspect list.

Sanchez reviewed the rest of the files, which took him until almost midnight. The story kept getting more interesting. The morning after Wally removed evidence, the tall figure reappeared and went into the shop. Not long after that, Wally, his nephew, and a dog appeared and also went into the building. About ten minutes later, Wally and Dan emerged, but the other man did not leave. Dan began to walk around as if he was searching and the dog started running in a circular pattern until it seemed to find something. Dan went to his truck and got a tablet computer then slowly walked indirectly toward the camera while looking at the screen of his tablet. Soon the dog zeroed in on the camera and you could see her jump up toward the lens, barking. Dan came and removed the camera. That is where the file ended. Each camera showed Dan as he walked around following the dog and retrieving the camera, stopping the recordings.

At the very least Wally and his nephew had gone into the garage where Willis was killed and removed evidence. Based on the last few files, it appeared as if they may either be working in partnership with the tall figure or may have possibly killed him. They seemed to all be in the shop at the same time. The key to all this would be to locate the files and binder removed from the garage, but it appeared as if the two Williamses committed one, possibly two, murders to obtain and/or protect that information. *What could a retired physicist have in his workshop that would motivate two deaths?*

Sanchez wrote up his notes, including a timeline of the events on the tapes. He called Thronson at home and woke him up to fill him in. They decided they would meet at eight o'clock to go up to the scene and arrest both Dan and Wally on suspicion of murder. He included in his notes that Wally had been reported missing but wondered if he had skipped town because he knew something about the incident. Sanchez informed Thronson he had not left any deputies to guard the site, but he would call Spinelli and tell him to head up immediately when his shift started at 6:00 a.m.

~ ~ ~ ~

Dan climbed into the cab of his truck and double-checked the contents. Besides his pistol, he noticed his cordless Dremel tool was missing from the console. It was the last resort if there were an emergency and Dan was unable to open a gate with the CDF key in his glove box. The car keys were not in the ignition, but he always kept a spare key in a hideaway box under his back bumper. After jumping out and retrieving the spare, he started the truck and turned on the headlights. Through the mist, he noticed both tracks and broken branches from a vehicle going straight through the brush. Dan turned off his truck and grabbed his flashlight, which was still wedged between the driver's seat and the console.

Ed heard the truck shut off and saw Dan climb out. He killed his engine and rolled down the window.

"What's the problem?"

"Looks like someone went hauling off through here but they wouldn't get far in that direction." Dan shined his flashlight on the path through the brush. "I hope it's the jerk who stole my truck."

He followed the path through the broken and crushed juniper bushes. The opening on the other side showed a ledge of rock barely large enough to stand on. Anyone who charged through this stuff

126

was in for a surprise. He could see the rear end and part of the bottom of a Jeep that had gone nose-first down into the boulders below. There was a National Car Rental license plate frame on the back. Dan chuckled to himself as he carefully made his way down the side of the drop-off, hopping from boulder to boulder. The wet rock was slippery, so Dan eased down the last few feet using his right hand on the Jeep to steady himself while holding the flashlight in his left hand.

He could see someone was still belted into the driver's seat. The driver's head moved slightly. Dan finally reached a boulder that put him level with the driver's window. He shined the flashlight inside.

"Nice job, dumbass." He was sure this was the person who stole his truck. The man in the Jeep did not move at first. Dan used the flashlight to scan the passenger compartment. Scattered on the dashboard was all of the surveillance equipment Dan had removed from the Willis place.

"What the heck?" About that time, Ed made it down to the boulder above Dan. He could see the person inside.

"Is he okay?"

"Not sure. I saw him move a minute ago." To the driver, "Hey, Pal, you alive in there?"

Dan tried the door, but it was jammed. Ed was able to open the rear door. The passenger groaned and moved his head again. When Ed opened the back door, the reflection of Dan's flashlight on the window lit the USGS logo on the Jeep. Dan was so focused on the window he had not noticed it before.

"Hey, this is the guy I saw in the back of the detective's car earlier," Ed said astonished. "How did he get here?" Ed was able to squeeze inside and pull the slumped driver back against the seat.

"Holy shit! He's been shot," Dan exclaimed. With the driver sitting back, Dan could see the entry wound in his shoulder. Then he saw the hole in the windshield.

"Well, the car doesn't seem to be in danger of catching fire." Ed looked at Dan. "Let's not move him. I'll run back to the house and call 911 so we can let the EMTs handle this. We could do more harm than good at this point."

"Okay, I'll stay with him."

Ed got out of the Jeep and made his way back to his truck. He started to pull away, but stopped and grabbed his rifle, got out again and returned to the edge. He climbed partway down, double-checked the safety and handed the gun to Dan by the barrel.

"Take this. We don't know what the hell is going on out here." After also tossing a bottle of water from his truck, he climbed up again. A minute later, Dan could hear his truck take off down the road in a hurry.

Dan climbed into the back seat to get out of the drizzle. He reached forward to gently recline the driver's seat so that he would not have the seatbelt pressing against the wound. Other than a few groans, the driver never moved or said anything. With the seat back nearly flat, he was held in place by the lower portion of the belt. This way Dan could access him and figured the EMTs could get him out of the rear door easier. Close to thirty minutes passed before Dan heard the wail of the sirens as the EMTs left the fire station across from Sam's Place.

Dan eventually crawled out of the vehicle because it was hard to sit with its nose down. He heard Ed's truck come to a stop on the road and some shouting as Ed directed the others where to find them. He relaxed a little then, as he figured all the commotion would definitely scare off the shooter if he were still around.

Ed appeared first at the top of the drop-off, followed closely by two young firemen. When their flashlights came across Dan standing there with a rifle, they were clearly shaken. The CDF rotated people in and out of the local station on a regular basis, so the locals usually did not get to know the firemen very well. They did not know Dan, and Ed only said something in passing about his nephew staying by the Jeep.

"I have this in case the shooter comes back." Dan set the rifle down and the EMTs relaxed. They moved efficiently, but Dan could see one of the men occasionally glancing over to ensure the gun was still on the ground.

"I'm gonna put this back in Ed's truck," Dan said loud enough for everyone to hear. He picked it up by the barrel so it would look less threatening.

"Here, I'll take that," Ed said to Dan, still standing at the top of the rocks. Dan handed the gun up to Ed after rechecking the safety. He listened to the paramedics describe the driver in their clinical tone.

"Victim is semiconscious with a gunshot wound to the left shoulder. He has a deep laceration on his forehead, likely to have a concussion…"

The voice droned on and Dan half tuned out. Then he heard, "Hey, this guy's an agent for the Department of Energy." One of the firemen had removed the driver's wallet to find identification and was holding a badge. "Special Agent Albert Stevens," he continued.

Dan was stunned, but now it made sense how he had the surveillance equipment, and why he was released by the sheriff's office. Could he have been the one to plant the cameras in the first place? If so, why? What does this have to do with Willis's murder?

Dan wasn't sure if they gave Stevens any drugs, but he suddenly heard him responding to the EMTs. After they assessed his injuries and determined there were no spinal complications, they began to pull him out of the rear door. Dan stepped up to assist and the agent opened his eyes, looking directly at him. The medic was trying to get an oxygen mask on, but Stevens used his one free hand to swipe it away.

"You have to give me those files back," he yelled, pointing at Dan.

"Get my equipment out of here. I can't leave without it. It's evidence." The last was directed at the firemen.

The EMT finally got the mask on him and he seemed to settle down a bit. Once they strapped him onto a stretcher, they began to hoist him up to the top of the rocks. They moved him into the ambulance and Dan could hear them call for a helicopter evacuation because he had lost a lot of blood. He could see through the rear ambulance doors Stevens's head was moving, going back and forth and from side to side. One of the firemen finally took the mask off so he could speak easier. Then they put it on again. One of the crew stepped out of the ambulance and walked over to Dan.

"He refuses to leave until we get his equipment out of the vehicle, and he insists you go with him." He shrugged his shoulders. "Could you gather up the stuff from the Jeep and meet us at the helo-pad by the station? I think the rain has eased up enough they can fly in."

"Sure." He climbed down the boulders and into the Jeep. Why did Stevens have a USGS sticker on the side if he was DOE? Dan found a box on the floor that must have contained the cameras. When he was sure he had everything from the Jeep, he climbed up and followed the ambulance to the fire station. The fire crew was so busy transferring the patient information it wasn't until the last minute they acknowledged Dan's presence. Dan handed the box to one of the firemen.

"He has to go too," was all they said to the flight crew, causing them to assume Dan worked with Stevens. They accommodated as best as they could. There was not a lot of room in the helicopter except for a small jump seat against the bulkhead. Dan had to squeeze in, which put him near Stevens's head on the right, while the medic was at his waist on the left, out of sight of the agent.

Dan wasn't sure what was going to happen to him, but he enjoyed the helicopter flight out of the valley at night. They gave Dan a headset so he could listen in, but the flight crew was relatively quiet.

He watched through a small window as the landing pad lights disappeared below, and saw the string of lights in bunches along Mines Road. Suddenly they cleared the cloud layer at the edge of the Diablo Range and the Silicon Valley opened up in front of them with a million lights and maze of highways and streets.

During the flight, the medical technicians in the medevac copter hooked Stevens up to an IV. Once they were pretty sure he did not have a concussion, they received permission from the hospital to give the patient a light dose of morphine to take the edge off the pain. That was when things changed drastically. The agent began mumbling, then suddenly he started talking as if in a conversation. At first, Dan was not sure to whom he was speaking. When Dan looked at Stevens, the morphine-laden agent was looking right at him, only inches away. Since Stevens could not see the others, he probably thought they were alone. Between the accident and the morphine, Dan suspected he had no idea where he was.

"I'm gonna need your full cooperation, Williams. Otherwise, I'll send your ass to Guantanamo."

Dan shook his head as if he didn't hear right.

"I can do that, you know. You don't know what you've stepped in, cowboy. I can say you're a domestic terrorist and hand you over to the FBI in a heartbeat."

Dan had no idea what he was getting at. "Okay, you have my full cooperation." Dan could think of nothing else to say.

"You ever in the military?"

"Marine Corps, sir, six years."

"Good. You thought you could screw with the DOE?" His words were starting to slur, so it sounded more like de-yo-we. "I keep track of our nuclear secrets, and you are up to your ass in alligators."

It was hard to take him seriously because Dan heard, "I kep trek of ar knuckler sucrits."

"The DOE has all the nukes." Stevens's breathing was more

pronounced now too. "We control all that shit. We monitor everybody, including retirees."

Dan could tell the agent was really buzzed now. He was surprised at how freely Stevens was talking. Dan had a Top Secret clearance in the Marine Corps, but he knew there were many levels above him based on some of the meetings he attended where there were lights that came on it the room indicating the clearance you needed to remain. He hoped what he heard would not land him in hot water somehow.

"What's this got to do with Willis?" Dan asked.

"Willis hit my radar before he retired. We always check finances. To see if they are a risk. And specialized knowledge too." His answers came in waves. "But Willis retired over twenty years ago."

Dan was surprised they would watch someone this long. "Did he do anything illegal or take bribes?"

"No. Willis was squeaky clean. But he was a Nazi expert during the war. He was the last of the Nazi gurus." Stevens paused. "Left a blind spot." The last word was almost inaudible.

Dan tried to think of something to keep him talking. "Willis was CIA?"

"Who said anything about CIA? Fuck the CIA."

His tone made Dan think he had pushed too far. He tried to backpedal. "Sorry, I thought they handled this kind of thing."

"I never said CIA. This is DOE shit."

"My mistake." Dan tried not to interrupt again.

Stevens was quiet for a few minutes. Dan was sure he had blown it, but maybe that was a good thing. This was quite a bit over his head. He looked back at the medic to see if they were listening, but the nurse closest to him was busy typing on the computer at her station.

"The In'nernet has made my job easier," Stevens finally said, almost wistfully.

"The Internet?"

The agent must have realized he was having trouble speaking. He slowed down his speech and tried to enunciate more. "Yup. Lots more tools now. We set traps. Know who is researching what. We get a flag. Bad guys come to us now."

"So that's how you caught on to activity around Willis?" Dan wasn't sure Stevens was still on the same subject now since Willis rarely used the Internet because he didn't trust it. Dan knew he was old school and preferred to go to a library rather than use Google. Perhaps he knew about his friends who were watching.

"Willis was bored. Started accessing Nazi shipping records looking for sunken treasure. Subs full of gold. Strike it rich before he croaked."

"How do you know this?"

"Have traps on all those records and research." Stevens sighed deeply, as if the drugs, or perhaps the weight of all he knew, were making him exhausted.

"But the Nazi research is over seventy years old now."

"Still some secrets, dunno why."

Stevens's breathing was getting heavier now. Dan wasn't sure how much he should push. He wanted to know everything but knew there could be some serious repercussions if others learned what he knew. Dan began to think Stevens had fallen asleep when he spoke again.

"The Nazis were exploring nuclear technology with the Japs. Swapping uranium for gold. Moved it in subs. Japs still don't know what all we found out. That shit is still closely guarded." Stevens's voice displayed excitement at the taboo topics. "The US tried to seize all their technology, Nazi bastards. We scrambled to get their nuclear scientists before the Russians did."

"I've read on the Internet about some strange aircraft the Nazis were developing." Dan was trying to keep him talking. "And they started using jet propulsion for both rockets and planes."

"Yeah, we were lucky the war ended. Bastards were prob'ly a year away from kickin' our ass." Stevens fell silent. "You ever hear of the Nazi Bell?"

It seemed random thoughts were being expressed now.

"Bits and pieces," Dan responded.

"There's lots of bullshit around that one."

"Yes, I saw a special about it on the History Channel. Some weird stuff," Dan admitted.

"'Nother way the In'nernet made my job simple." Stevens laughed. "Sprinkle bits of truth with lots of bullshit. We have a whole section of folks who put misinformation out on the Internet to confuse the Chinese and Russians. If you search for Nazi Bell, you get sent down a rabbit hole. Same for time travel bullshit."

"So it's all bullshit?" Dan had seen pieces about the Bell being a time travel machine, and stories about the Philadelphia Experiment. He liked to watch them for their entertainment value but took it with a grain of salt.

"What? Time travel? Hell yes, it's bullshit, but that's where your buddy Willis comes in. He knew more about what the Nazis were doing in physics than anyone. Was in the Army in the war and translated documents from the Nazis. S'how he ended up at Livermore Labs."

"Was he the expert on time travel or something?"

"He helped debunk most of it. Stuff pops up every once in a while. We encourage it. Adds misinformation." Stevens laughed to himself. "But time travel has taken on a life of its own. Some whackos continued to pursue it. General Peron built a physics lab in Bariloche, in Argentina, for Nazis there supposedly trying to chase it. General Kammler was tracked to Argentina. So was his money guy, Bormann."

"But those guys must be long gone by now." Dan figured they would have to be in their nineties at least.

"Yes, but there's still a few hardcore believers hanging on. Relatives or descendants who hope the Nazi Empire rises from the ashes."

Dan could hear a few deep breaths before he continued.

"We watched them, shared with the CIA pricks. They're not viable. But we noticed chatter recently involving Willis. Seems he was close to locating some long-lost subs full of gold. Started pinging some folks in South America, even went down there once. Raised the flag to monitor him."

"But it wasn't you who hurt Willis, to shut him up?"

"No. No. I'm just a surveillance guy." Stevens shook his head. "I don't do that shit. I'd call in a team. We'd bring him in for a come-to-Jesus-meeting to scare him. We threaten prison, take his pension."

"So what the hell happened to Willis?"

"Don't know. Saw you and your uncle taking stuff. Thought you had a beef with Willis. Land dispute or shum'body shot shum'body's dog." He paused. "What'd your uncle take?"

"Well, we found a hidden room that must have been his secret library. Wally grabbed what was on the desk, thinking maybe that was what Willis was working on."

"Waz in it?"

"I have no idea. I only looked through it briefly. The documents were in German and appeared to have a Nazi insignia on them. Neither one of us can read a lick of German."

"Where are they now?" Stevens sounded a bit more alert.

"We hid them until we could turn them over to the sheriff. But they got so bent out of shape about me being on the property that I was afraid to mention it."

"We suspected Willis might have taken some papers with him when he left. Couldn't prove it. Bad idea for you to take them."

"I know, but it was probably a good thing we did. When we went back for Wally to show me where he got them, someone had been there. I assumed it was you." Dan was hoping he wasn't digging a deeper hole for himself and Wally.

"Wasn't me. But I want to see this room. You need to get those documents to me pronto. Could be dangerous for you. Guy who shot me was a head taller than you." More heavy breathing came through the headphones. "That gold would be worth a fortune now."

"Do you think someone is trying to get to Willis's information?"

"You saw the house broken into. There's a guy on the tape. You came later. No way to tell who it was. Too far away from the camera." He took another deep breath. "I need those files. You get 'em to me, we're good, Williams."

Dan felt the helicopter descending and realized they were landing at the hospital. There was a flurry of activity around the agent as he was ushered inside. Dan followed, carrying the box of equipment. As he entered the emergency room, he heard a voice behind him.

"Agent?"

Dan looked around, but no one else was near. He turned toward the nurse, who was motioning for him to come to the counter. "Can you help us with the paperwork for your friend?"

"Sorry. I'm not an agent, but I can tell you what I know."

She frowned and hesitated. "The flight crew said—"

"Things were kinda hectic when they picked us up. I live up there, and they asked me to collect this equipment. Is there a sheriff's department person or a policeman I can leave this with? It's important to the agent. Evidence."

The nurse picked up the phone and called to check if there were any sheriff's personnel available. There was, but since they had flown into the Castro Valley Trauma Center, it was an Alameda County officer instead of Santa Clara County. When a deputy arrived, Dan explained the situation and turned over the box of equipment. He worried about handing everything over but remembered he copied all the files onto his computer at home and could use those to see if he could identify the intruder.

He called a friend of his that lived a few towns away. By the time Dan's friend picked him up, it was one o'clock in the morning. Dan turned down the offer of crashing at his friend's house but did ask if he could borrow a vehicle to get home. He was worried about his uncle and the fact that someone was running around shooting people. Dan's friend let him borrow a truck.

It was three-thirty by the time Dan got home. There was still no sign of Syd, but Dan was too exhausted to do anything except call for her a few times outside. He finally stumbled into the bedroom and fell face-first onto the bed, still dressed, sound asleep.

CHAPTER 14 - SATURDAY, MAY 15TH

Deputy Spinelli had trouble waking up Saturday morning after being called in the middle of the night. Sanchez did not tell him much, other than to get up to the crime scene and secure it first thing. Spinelli stopped and picked up two large coffees to jolt himself awake. With the twisty roads, he did not get much of a chance to sip as he made his way up the mountain. It was a little after seven when Spinelli reached the crime scene. Everything looked secure, so he sat in his cruiser enjoying his coffee. The air was pleasantly cool up in the hills and there was a quiet you couldn't get in the city or the suburbs. He rolled down his window and tried to relax. The only noise was the occasional Steller's Jay scolding a squirrel as they both vied for the same acorn. He heard the police radio crackle now and then, but reception was limited up here and he did not have the needed whip antennae Thronson had on his SUV. He climbed out of the car and leaned against the fender to get away from the radio static.

He could hear an occasional yip that sounded like a dog, but far away. Maybe there was a coyote den somewhere on the ridge. He listened carefully, thinking he might see some coyote pups. He knew they were a nuisance to the locals, but the young ones were cute. It sounded like it was coming from behind the shop. Spinelli figured it would probably be a good idea to check out the perimeter anyway, so he walked in that direction. When he got to the rear of the shop, he could see a wellhead covered by a small structure not much bigger than a large doghouse. It looked like something was digging near it, as there was a good-sized mound of loose dirt thrown around in front of the structure.

A sudden yip and spray of dirt shot out of the hole. Spinelli approached the wellhead cautiously and looked into the hole. Down about three feet, Dan's dog was at the bottom, panting and looking darn near exhausted. It got up and threw another spray of dirt between its back legs. The dog must have heard Spinelli because it looked up and scrambled out of the hole. The poor thing looked as if it had been digging all night to get that deep. Spinelli always liked animals and felt sorry for the exhausted-looking pooch.

"Come, boy, come on. Good dog." Spinelli tried coaxing, but it must have remembered him from the other day because it trotted about twenty feet away and sat down facing him. When he approached, it gave a short growl and moved another twenty feet away, sitting down again. Spinelli tried several times, but the dog kept eluding in a circle to stay close to the hole. It sat there staring at him, panting and looking tired.

Spinelli went to his cruiser and took out a bottle of water and one of his empty coffee cups. When he returned the dog was in the hole again, but it shot out as it heard him approach. Spinelli poured some water into the cup and placed it near the hole, then walked away about thirty feet from the hole. The dog eyed him nervously. It slowly approached the offering and sniffed it. After a few seconds, it took one lap of water as if to test it. Once it was satisfied, the dog began lapping up the water but kept its eyes glued to Spinelli. Spinelli tried to feed it some turkey from a sandwich he brought to eat for lunch, but the dog would not touch the food. It sat there watching him, protecting the hole.

Spinelli knew it was pointless trying to get the dog to trust him, so decided to get some help and returned to his cruiser. He could not raise Thronson on the radio and decided to try driving over to the Rockin' A. It was only a few miles so he should be back before the others arrived.

At the Rockin' A there was no activity around the house. No cars or trucks were in the driveway or under the covered parking at the front, and there was no response to his knock on the door. The dog's behavior worried him, so he decided to try Hawk's Nest.

Maybe they were moving cattle or something. The drive down there would take about twenty minutes, so he attempted again to raise Thronson on the radio. No answer.

Spinelli had only been on the other part of the ranch once, but he knew there were at least two gates he would need to get through. He remembered there was a pay phone outside Sam's Place, so he drove to the restaurant. When Spinelli picked up the receiver, there was no dial tone. As he walked back to his cruiser, he heard his cell phone chime to indicate he received an email. That meant he must have service.

He pulled out the phone and sure enough it had two bars. He called directory assistance and asked for Dan Williams's number. The operator connected him, and soon the line was ringing.

☐

~ ~ ~ ~

Dan was not sure he was ever asleep when the phone started ringing. He looked at the clock—He'd only been asleep three hours. If this was anyone other than Wally, they were a dead person. It took him a few seconds to comprehend the voice on the other end of the line. Syd? Huh?

"Wait. Start over again. I was asleep."

"Dan, I think your dog is at the crime scene. He's been digging for what looks like hours and is acting weird."

"Who is this?"

"Sorry, it's Deputy Spinelli. When I got up there this morning I heard a dog. I went to look and he was down in a hole, digging. He won't let me near him."

"Where is this?"

"At the Willis place."

"Okay. Okay. Let me get dressed, and I'll be right there. But you should know Syd's a girl."

Dan hung up and shook his head to clear the cobwebs. He didn't want to take time for a shower, so he ran his head under cold water to wake himself up. Still dressed from the night before, Dan stumbled out to his truck tugging on a light jacket. He pulled up to the Willis property a record fifteen minutes later. Spinelli was out of his car and pointed behind the shop. Dan drove around to the rear, and as soon as Syd heard the familiar diesel, she was out of the hole and greeting Dan at the door of his truck. She barked excitedly and ran back to the hole.

"What's up, Syd? What is it, girl?"

Dan and Spinelli walked up to the hole and looked down. It looked like she was digging against a concrete wall. Dan ran to his pickup and grabbed a shovel out of the back. He went to the hole and started digging along the concrete to see how wide it was. It was at least four feet wide, and the dog had dug down nearly four feet in places. Dan stood up.

"This can't be a wellhead. It's too big. I haven't seen anyone up here pour this much concrete for a well." He began looking closer at the enclosure at the top, trying to find a way to open it.

"You think it's a root cellar or something?" Spinelli walked around the structure looking at it.

"No, I don't." Dan stood and looked at the rear of the shop. He got up and paced it off. "That room," he said, referring to the secret room below the shop, "is about forty feet long, made from an old cargo container. This is close to fifty feet." He was talking to himself.

"What room? What are you talking about?"

Dan held up his palm to indicate for Spinelli to wait. "This is the escape exit. That's how he got away!"

"Who got away? What the hell are you talking about, damn it?" Spinelli was losing his patience.

"There's got to be a latch or a door here." Dan was now kneeling down looking at the structure covering the wellhead.

Spinelli grabbed his shoulder. "Dan?"

"Look. Wally found a secret room under the rear of the shop. When we looked at it, there was a hatch at the far end that was probably an escape exit. It would be about here, so this must be the disguised cover for it." As he said this, he slid his hand under the edge of the building and found a lever. When he pulled it, the whole structure tilted up revealing a metal ladder mounted inside a concrete tunnel in the ground.

Spinelli shined his flashlight down into the tunnel. They could see some work boots at the bottom of the shaft. Dan closed his eyes and leaned against the upright cover, feeling a bit woozy at the sight of his uncle's boots that he recognized at the bottom of the shaft. When he regained some control and opened them again, the boots moved. His breath caught, then he went into action.

"Uncle, we're here. Hang on. We're coming down." He started down the ladder without a light or a plan other than to get to his uncle.

Spinelli started down right after him. When they got to the bottom, they had to stoop over. The room had solid concrete walls and was probably ten feet by ten feet and about four feet high. There were some supplies, including bottled water and canned goods, along one side with a camping stove and bedding. There was a hatch-like door Dan assumed led to the hidden room. This must have been a storage/safe room/escape route.

Wally was on his side, trussed up like a Christmas turkey. When Dan put his hand on his uncle's shoulder, Wally began kicking and writhing to get away. Dan loosened his gag and noticed the earplugs. Wally gasped for air once the gag was removed but still couldn't see because his eyes were not adjusted to the light yet. With the earplugs out, Dan got him calmed down enough to begin untying his hands and legs.

"Are you alright, Uncle? Man, we were worried about you."

"Stop your screaming will you and get that damned light out of my face." Wally leaned against the wall gasping for breath from the exertion of trying to get away. His legs and arms were still too numb to control them.

Dan realized what was going on and started massaging them to get the circulation going again. As soon as Syd heard Wally's voice, she began yelping and put her paws on the wall of the tunnel and looked over it.

Spinelli noticed the gash on the back of Wally's head and tried to examine it as best as he could. "This looks pretty bad. We need to get you to a hospital."

Wally winced at the pain and. Spinelli noticed his eyes were not focusing well.

Dan opened the hatch to the main room and crawled through. He found the light switch and turned on the lights. They gently moved Wally to the study and placed him in the recliner to make him more comfortable. After giving him some of the water from the storage room, Spinelli went to his cruiser to call for help. He could not reach the dispatcher, but Thronson, who was on his way, responded this time and relayed the message to the dispatcher. Thronson ordered Spinelli to remain where he was and to detain Dan and to send someone with Wally if he didn't beat the helicopter.

Downstairs, Wally could not remember what had happened to him or how he ended up in that room. After drinking some water and eating a bit of a granola bar Spinelli had with him, he began to come around a little.

"Syd found you. She must have been digging all night to get to you," Dan said.

Dan went up the stairs and slid the plywood out of the way. He rolled the pegboard aside and moved the toolbox from where he was on the stairs. Syd was already there, waiting. As soon as she saw an opening, Syd ran down the stairs straight to Wally, licking his hand that hung over the arm of the chair. Wally grabbed the dog and hugged her neck close to him while Syd planted wet kisses on his face. Usually not one to tolerate canine affection, Wally smiled and continued hugging. When they finally broke from the embrace, Wally fell back in the chair.

"There is no doubt about it. That is the smartest damned dog in the world. C'mer, Syd."

And with that, Syd jumped in his lap and continued to lick his chin.

~ ~ ~ ~

After taking the call from Spinelli and relaying the need for a medevac, Thronson received another call from headquarters on his phone. He was surprised when his phone rang, as he was up in the hills near Sam's Place. Thronson pulled the SUV into the small parking lot so they wouldn't lose the signal. When he hung up, he looked over at Sanchez, who was riding with him.

"Looks like we have to take a very short detour," Thronson announced.

Sanchez looked at him with a frown.

They pulled out of Sam's Place and went north on Mines Road about two hundred yards, then turned into the CDF fire station. The fire captain came out to meet them. Captain Dave O'Shea was a soft-spoken man who stood about five foot ten. He had the shoulders and arms of a man who worked out regularly and thinning brown hair. The most notable thing about him though was his striking blue eyes, which contrasted with his dark hair.

"Hey, thanks for the fast response." He smiled and shook both men's hands. As they exchanged names, the ambulance took off out of its bay.

"They're headed to your murder site," the captain said when they could hear again.

"Yeah, I called it in. EMTs need to stabilize Wally Williams until the medevac gets here. Let them know we want someone to go with him until we figure out what's going on here. I already told my deputy who's on the scene."

O'Shea got on the radio and relayed the additional information. When he returned, Thronson spoke first.

"What's this about?"

"We had to medevac someone else last night. That guy Stevens. I guess he's a fed."

"What happened to the little jerk? He sure made a stink at our headquarters. Was he taking video of somebody's wife?" Thronson smiled at his own joke.

"He was shot and crashed his Jeep down by the Drop-Off."

"Really? What time? He didn't leave the jail until eight o'clock last night," Sanchez said.

"It was around ten-thirty or eleven when we got the call. The thing is, Dan Williams was on the scene." O'Shea paused. "And he had a rifle."

"Oh, for Christ's sake. We're going to need to open a substation up here soon." Thronson stood up and started pacing. He thought better on his feet. "Who called it in?"

"Nobody. Ed Wyath, his uncle, drove here to get us," the captain answered.

"You think Ed witnessed the shooting?" Sanchez interjected.

"No idea. We were too busy getting Stevens out and stable to ask a lot of questions. But the agent, or whatever he is, insisted Dan go with him but I'm not sure that means he was taken into custody."

"We'll have to check with Stevens?" Thronson said.

"The Life Flight usually takes patients to the trauma center in Castro Valley, so it probably hasn't gotten relayed from Alameda County Sheriff's Office yet. When I heard that you called this morning, I thought you should know."

"Thanks." Then, looking at Sanchez, "We'd better get over there."

~ ~ ~ ~

Dan could hear sirens coming down the road, so he went up to the shop door to guide the EMTs down to his Wally. He did not want to try to carry him up the stairs until they checked him out. Wally was lucid but weak. When the EMTs got out of the ambulance, they looked surprised to see Dan again.

"Follow me," Dan directed the EMTs. "Wally's downstairs." He went ahead of them. The EMTs went right to work evaluating Wally, and Dan could tell they were concerned about the head wound.

"What's his name?" one of the EMTs asked Spinelli.

"Hey, I'm right here, asshole. My name is Wally Williams." Wally was irritated that they were treating him as if he were clueless.

"Wally, do you know what day it is?" The EMT was going through the standard questions for evaluating concussions.

"Listen, butthead, I just spent what seemed like several days tied up in a dark room with my eyes covered and my ears plugged. So I'd say it's my lucky day."

"What day of the week is it, Wally?" he tried again.

"I just told you, I don't know! I was in a sensory deprivation chamber. You try that for a few days and get back to me on what day you think it is." Wally was hot now.

"Okay, okay, calm down. We're gonna get you taken care of."

Dan put his hand on the EMT's shoulder. "Hey, Uncle, what's my

147

birthday?"

"July thirtieth. Why, did somebody hit you in the head too?" Wally shot back.

Dan laughed. "He's okay."

The EMTs determined Wally was dehydrated, so started him on fluids and began to put him on a narrow wooden stretcher so they could transport him up the stairs. As they were loading him into the ambulance, Dan could see Thronson's SUV coming onto the property.

Spinelli stepped forward to talk to the EMTs. "I was told that I have to accompany the victim. He is likely going to be charged with obstruction, and possibly murder." He sounded apologetic.

"What? Are you kidding me?" Dan put himself between Spinelli and the gurney.

"Come on, Dan. You know I don't believe it either, but I've been ordered to accompany him."

The EMT stepped between them. "You'll have to take it up with the Life Flight guys. You can follow us to the helo-pad."

Thronson pulled up and opened his door.

Dan was in his face before he got out of the SUV. "What the heck is the idea of arresting my uncle after what he has just been through? Doesn't the fact that someone knocked him out and left him tied up, prove he's not the bad guy here?" Dan was so mad the veins on his forehead were standing out.

"Dan Williams. I'm surprised to see you back up here already." Thronson looked over at Spinelli with an aggravated look. Spinelli forgot to mention Williams was with him. "Didn't Agent Stevens arrest you last night?"

"He didn't arrest me. Just asked that I gather his equipment so it wouldn't be lost." Dan stepped back and took a deep breath. He was surprised by Thronson's attitude. "I turned it over to a deputy at the hospital."

"Not from what I've been told." Thronson reached behind him on his belt and came out with handcuffs. "Now why don't you put your hands on the hood there and settle down."

"What?" Dan was in utter disbelief. "What are you charging me with?"

"Every time there is a problem up here, you seem to be around. So for now I'm just going to take you in to explain yourself. But don't push it because I can think of several possibilities. There's attempted murder of a federal officer, assault with a deadly weapon, tampering with evidence, obstruction of a sheriff's department investigation and accessory to murder, to start with."

"Whoa, whoa, whoa! I haven't done any of those things."

"Detective, read him his rights. Let's keep him where we can see him until we talk to Stevens." Sanchez cuffed Dan's hands behind his back as Sanchez droned the Miranda rights.

"I'd suggest you keep your mouth shut," Sanchez said in Dan's ear when he finished the speech.

"Deputy, I need you to secure this scene. I can have someone meet the helicopter at the hospital," Thronson said to Spinelli.

He shoved Dan in the rear seat of the SUV. Before Dan could even collect his thoughts, the ambulance headed out the dirt road and Thronson pulled the SUV in behind to follow them.

Overhead, the Life Flight crew was circling the Willis ranch looking for a closer place to land when they saw the ambulance and sheriff's SUV heading toward the road. They contacted the ambulance via radio and coordinated the pickup at the CDF landing pad. Circling once more, they headed north to the fire station.

~ ~ ~ ~

Spinelli stood watching the procession disappear into the distance and the helicopter circle overhead. Syd started to run after the SUV but lay down after a short distance. She had not recovered from her long night of digging.

Spinelli walked over to her and stroked the dog's head. "It's gonna be okay, girl." It was the first time Syd let him near her without growling. He went to his cruiser and grabbed a sandwich, took the meat off and offered it to her. To his surprise, she took the offer.

When Spinelli's replacement arrived in the afternoon, he coaxed Syd into the front seat of the squad car and headed over to the Rockin' A. He didn't want to leave her alone in her weakened condition, and could think of nowhere else to take her. He recognized Mrs. Wyatt's car in the driveway after seeing her at the murder scene the other day. When Syd jumped out of the car she was greeted by Rounder, who did not even bark at Spinelli since he was with Syd.

Margaret came around the side of the house. "I thought I heard somebody pull in." A serious look crossed her face. "Is everything alright?"

"Yes, ma'am," Spinelli tried to smile to reassure her. "Sort of."

She waited for him to speak first.

"We found Wally. He's okay, but he has a nasty bump on his head. That was him on the helicopter earlier."

"I got home about an hour ago. I was visiting my sister in Oroville." She looked concerned again. "I didn't know Wally was missing. What happened?"

Spinelli started to fill her in on the details, but she insisted they get a cold drink and sit down on the back patio where it was cooler. He told her about Wally's disappearance and how they found him. Syd lay under the picnic table where they were sitting, and when she heard her name being used she walked over and put her head on Margaret's lap.

"Good girl, Syd. We'll need to get you something special for a reward." She stroked the dog's head as she spoke.

"The other news is not so good. Thronson has arrested Dan." He tried to break it as gently as he could. "I'm sure we'll get it all cleared up, but Thronson took him in again this morning."

"For what?" She couldn't believe her ears. Dan would never do anything that would be worth arresting him.

Spinelli had to start at the part where Dan found the cameras and saw a face on the screen. "When they caught the guy in the video, it turned out he was a federal agent so was released within a few hours. He came back up here then someone shot him."

"Well, surely Thronson doesn't think Dan did that," she said in disbelief.

"When the EMTs showed up at the scene, Dan had a rifle. It kinda freaked them out so they told Thronson."

"Was the wound from a rifle?" Margaret asked.

"I don't think we know yet. Dan said he was with Ed when they found the agent, so we need to talk to Ed too."

"He should be home anytime now. He needed to go to the Valley early this morning about some property in Merced we're selling. I'll let him know what's going on."

"Thank you, ma'am. And thank you for the iced tea. You take care of Syd now. She's one heck of a dog."

"That she is, and thanks for bringing her over."

~ ~ ~ ~

Paulo was awakened by the sound of a helicopter flying overhead. He was startled and disoriented, and also surprised he had slept so late in the back seat, where he didn't fit all that well. He lay there until he heard the helicopter circle several times and then fly off. *Were they looking for him?* Unsure whether he or the Jeep were spotted, he peered over the front seats and listened for any vehicles coming. He thought he heard one car on the road, but fortunately it kept going.

Looking around at his surroundings he noticed he was about a quarter of a mile from what appeared to be a cabin along a dirt track. Beside it, he could see a crude carport with a dirt bike sitting beneath it, which he had not been able to see in the storm the night before. Paulo tucked the gun into his belt behind his back and climbed out of the Jeep. He was stiff from lying in a fetal position all night. After stretching a bit, he walked over to the cabin. There was no use making noise by starting the Jeep.

The motorcycle was a Honda dirt bike made street legal and even had a valid license plate on it. It was secured to a post by a bicycle cable and lock. He wished he thought to bring the Dremel tool. Paulo looked in a shed behind the cabin and found a power generator. There was an oversized screwdriver sitting beside it on the floor. He took the screwdriver and used it to pry open one of the windows in the rear of the cabin. Once inside he found bottled water, some crackers and a glass container of jerky. The saltines were stale but filled his gnawing stomach. In one closet he discovered a small toolbox with a set of bolt cutters he could use to cut the chain on the motorcycle. They would save him from having to go back to his Jeep for the Dremel. He also found a helmet and a jacket on a shelf in the closet. It was a bit tight, and the sleeves were a little short, but he could use it.

He went out to the bike and was able to cut the cable. Looking in a small pouch on the rear fender he found a tire repair kit, including some compressed air canisters. The gas tank was almost full, and after a few kicks the bike sputtered to life. Since it was a dirt bike with only a kill switch button to turn off the engine, it didn't need a key. Paulo grew up riding similar bikes back home in Argentina on his grandfather's ranch.

He rode down to the Jeep and let some air out of the rear tire on the driver's side and moved the spare over into some bushes. The low tire would be his excuse for borrowing the bike if Paulo ran into someone at the cabin when he returned. He could refill the tire with the air canisters.

Paulo made his way to the road and opened the gate, putting the lock in place so the cut was not evident when he closed it. He couldn't tell if a lot of people used the dirt road because the rain had eliminated any tracks. His were the only set in the new layer of mud. He hoped he had at least one day before anyone returned to the cabin. That should be all he needed. The helmet and change of vehicle would also ensure he was anonymous if it was him for whom the helicopter was searching.

Paulo needed to get into town to pick up a few things before he paid a visit to that ranch again. To his surprise, a group of motorcycles came past as he was mounting the dirt bike. It was a group of sport bikes, but not far behind them were some dual-sport motorcycles. It occurred to him it was Saturday and this road would be popular with motorcyclists on the weekends. Perfect. It made it even easier to blend in. He fell in a quarter mile behind the dual-sport group.

Michael L. Patton

CHAPTER 15 - SATURDAY AFTERNOON

After the ride into town, Dan was placed in an interrogation room, still handcuffed and famished. He realized he hadn't eaten since lunch the day before. He pleaded with the deputy guarding him until they finally brought him a can of Coke and a package of peanut butter crackers from the vending machine. The deputy released his handcuffs from being locked to a ring on the table, but didn't take them off. It was a bit of a struggle for Dan to open the package and drink. It was another two hours before Thronson and Sanchez showed up. When they walked in, Sanchez sat down across from Dan, while Thronson stood with his back to the wall near the doorway.

"Let me guess." He pointed to Sanchez. "You're the good cop, and he's the bad cop."

Sanchez glared at him. "Don't be a wise guy. I don't think you know how much trouble you're in here."

"Wait. Let's take this one by one. Okay?" Dan leaned forward in his chair.

"You're waving your right to an attorney?"

"For now. Because I didn't do anything." He held his arms out palms up as best he could with the handcuffs in a pleading gesture. "Let's see how this goes. I can invoke my rights at any time, right?" He looked from one to the other.

"Yes," both men said together.

"Okay. Agent Stevens. He was already shot when Ed and I found him."

"So, Mr. Wyatt was with you yesterday evening?" Sanchez started writing notes.

"He was when we found the agent. He took me to my truck."

"Where was your truck?" This time it was Thronson asking.

"It was stolen a few hours before that."

Sanchez looked up from his writing. "How did Mr. Wyatt know where it was?"

"He saw it beside the road when he was coming home. Listen, I was looking for my uncle. I went to the Rockin' A to talk to Ed, but he wasn't there. So I went to the shop to do some work while I waited for him."

"What time was this?" Sanchez interrupted.

"It was about an hour before dark."

"So, around seven-thirty?"

"Somewhere around then. I was working in the shop and I thought I heard a car door. When I looked out of the shop someone was in my truck."

"And what time was this?"

"It was just getting dark because he hit me with the headlights and I couldn't tell who it was." Dan thought for a minute. "I could tell he was tall though by how close he came to the roof of the truck. I could see the outline of someone. I ran out of the shop and tried to block him, but he took off straight up the hill through the barbed wire fence and down the road, toward Mt. Hamilton."

"That would have been around eight-thirty?" Sanchez clarified.

"I guess so."

"Did you report it?" Thronson asked as he moved away from the wall.

"I tried to, but the phones up there were out. It was pouring. They go out if we get enough rain for the lines to get wet," Dan explained

"Well, that's convenient." Thronson leaned back against the wall again, but he knew it was likely in those rural areas.

Dan shook his head.

"And when did Mr. Wyath show up?"

Dan could see Sanchez was drawing a timeline on his notepad.

"It must have been around nine-thirty. Ed scared the crap out of me. Came in the door with a gun drawn because he didn't see my truck outside."

"Was that the rifle you had when the EMTs saw you?" Thronson pulled away from the wall each time he asked a question.

"No. It was a different one."

"Jesus. You cowboys and your guns." Thronson asked and started pacing.

"We have enough to protect ourselves. When I told Ed my truck was stolen he said he'd seen it down the road. I guess the guy drove it to where he parked and searched through it. Ed took me to it. It was probably a quarter to ten when we got there." Dan anticipated the question that time and Sanchez added it to his timeline.

"Was anything taken?" Thronson stopped midstride.

"Yes. My nine-millimeter pistol and a cordless Dremel cutoff tool I keep in the console." Dan had to turn partially to answer Thronson, who had walked behind him. He wished the guy would sit down and stop pacing.

"Oh, for Pete's sake!" Thronson exclaimed in reaction to the mention of another gun.

"How far away was your truck parked from the shop?"

"About three miles or so."

Sanchez tried to summarize. "So according to your own estimate of the timeline, you had the entire evening to shoot the agent and walk back to the shop, where you waited for Ed and came up with some story about your truck being stolen."

"Why would I park Wally's truck there too?" Dan was feeling off balance now. "And have you even determined the type of bullet he was shot with? We don't even know if it was a rifle or a pistol."

"You had both in your possession, didn't you?" Thronson leaned on the far end of the table.

"But do you know what it was?" Dan insisted.

"No. We're waiting for a report from the Alameda County Sheriff's Department," Sanchez admitted.

"The car's engine was still warm when Ed and I got there." Dan was desperately searching for something to prove he couldn't have done it.

"Where is Ed? We tried to contact him." Thronson was looking through his notes as he made another pass around the room.

"He mentioned on the way to my truck yesterday that he needed to go to Merced about some property they're selling. He probably left early this morning." Dan desperately wished he was here now to back him up. These guys are gaining momentum in the wrong direction.

"What happened next?" Sanchez held his pencil poised to extend his timeline.

"I checked to see what was missing, and when I started to leave I saw the path through the brush where the Cherokee went. I knew there was a drop-off right there, so I went to look. That's when we saw the agent's car." Dan tried to maintain eye contact with Sanchez.

"You wait until you have a witness, then you discover the Jeep. That's convenient too." The Wandering Lieutenant was pacing again.

Dan gave him an annoyed look. "Why would I try to save him if I was the one who shot him?" Dan bristled.

"Maybe you were sure he would already be dead," Thronson shot back.

"Have you talked to Agent Stevens yet? He can clear me. He said the guy was quite a bit taller than me."

"No, we have not questioned Stevens," Sanchez admitted.

"Maybe you were standing on a rock. It's hard to judge height when someone is shooting at you," Thronson insisted.

"Oh, for God's sake." Dan tried to throw up his hands, but the handcuffs prevented it.

After a few minutes of silence, Sanchez tried to get Dan back on track. "The EMTs said you went on the Life Flight with the agent. Is that correct?"

"Yes." Dan was afraid to dig himself deeper by volunteering any more details.

"Why?" Sanchez stopped writing and leaned closer to Dan as he asked.

"The EMTs told me Agent Stevens was insisting I gather the equipment from his car and go with him."

"This is the surveillance equipment you took from the Willis property?" Sanchez clarified.

"Yes. It was still in Stevens's car and he wanted to keep it in his custody." Dan closed his eyes as he tried to remember what exactly was said.

A meaty palm slammed down on the table causing Dan to jump and open his eyes.

"We'll get back to you removing equipment later. Did Stevens take you into custody?" Thronson asked, thinking about how the fire captain worded the description earlier.

"No. He never said that," Dan snapped back. Getting control of himself, he added, "I assumed he needed me to carry it and keep track of it until we could find someone to turn it over to."

"Is that what you did?" Thronson was the Wandering Lieutenant again.

"When I got to the hospital I found a sheriff's deputy and turned everything over, yes."

"And then you left?" Thronson was incredulous.

"Yes. The agent was in surgery and I turned everything over to the deputy. I was not in custody so I assumed my civic duty was complete and I left."

"Did someone pick you up?" Thronson asked.

"A friend of mine who lives down that way picked me up and let me borrow his truck to get home."

"What time was that?" It was the timekeeper again.

"Around 1:00 a.m. I didn't get home until three-thirty or so. I crashed until Spinelli's call woke me up a little after seven I think."

Dan was afraid to say anything about the conversation with the agent during the flight. He was worried they would add terrorism or something else to the list of charges. Dan tried to calm himself, realizing Thronson's pacing and badgering were meant to keep him off balance.

He took a deep breath and said calmly, "You should definitely talk to Agent Stevens. We talked a little, and I think he might have some theories on Willis's murder."

"What do you mean?" Thronson asked, leaning on the table again.

"Well, it was hard to figure out if it was the drugs talking or a real theory. Stevens mentioned something about Willis being an expert on Nazi weapons and gold shipments and people became interested in what he knew. I don't know." Dan felt panic rising up thinking he said too much.

"Can we confirm this with the flight crew? Did they hear it?" Thronson pressed.

"No. For some reason, the crew thought I was Stevens's partner or something, so they set up a separate channel for us to talk."

"Separate channel?" Sanchez looked confused.

"On the headphones. You need them to hear each other in the helicopter."

Sanchez nodded his head, but Dan wasn't sure he got it. He saw Sanchez write a note to follow-up. Sanchez stood up from his chair.

"Okay, let's take a break. I need to check a few things," Sanchez said as both men spun around and left the room.

Dan's panic turned into a tidal wave.

~ ~ ~ ~

Ed was not in the best of moods when he finally got to the ranch. He got up early to drive to Merced and spent over two hours sitting in a meeting listening to two lawyers argue over the obscure points of a real estate contract, the result of which would be less money than they charged for the time they spent bickering. His partner, Bob, was in the middle of a heated divorce. Ed recommended Bob talk to his soon-to-be-ex spouse and figure it out because the two idiots in the room were doing their best to chew through his share before they even sold it. He turned and left the room in spite of a lot of guffawing on the part of the two attorneys.

He had no better luck when he stopped at the Chevrolet dealer in Modesto on the way back to see if the water pump he'd ordered for one of their older trucks came in. He knew it was due today and hoped he wouldn't have to make another trip into town to pick it up. When the parts guy checked the computer, it showed it would be delivered later in the afternoon. To keep it from being a total wasted trip, he treated himself to a burrito at his favorite Mexican place for an early lunch.

When he returned to the ranch, Margaret greeted him with the news that Dan was arrested and charged with shooting the federal agent and a multitude of other crimes. She didn't have all the details but told him a deputy named Spinelli brought Syd to the ranch and they had a really nice chat.

"Spinelli? Really? Oh for the love of…" He walked into the den and picked up the phone. When he got the sheriff's department, he asked for Lieutenant Thronson. After five minutes on hold, Thronson came on the line.

"Lieutenant Thronson here."

"Thronson? This is Ed Wyath. What the hell do you people think you're doing arresting my nephew?"

"Well, Mr. Wyath, I understand your concern but I'm really not at liberty to discuss the details with you. I can tell you we have some pretty compelling evidence."

"My understanding is you have charged him with the shooting of the man we found last night up here at the Drop-Off. I can tell you we discovered him together."

"I understand that Mr. Wyath, but there are significant amounts of time where no one can corroborate his whereabouts so it would give him enough opportunity."

"I can tell you he couldn't have shot him with my rifle the EMTs saw because I had it with me until I gave it to him."

"We haven't got the report back telling us what kind of gun was used, but I am not about to believe the cockamamie story your nephew told about Nazi gold and that he and Agent Stevens were working together. He said they had a heart-to-heart on the copter ride and everything is cleared up."

"Why in God's name would he leave his own truck at the scene where he shot a federal officer? When I found him in the shop, he was busy working. If I had shot a fed, I would get in my truck and get the heck out of Dodge."

"That's good to know, Mr. Wyath. Maybe he panicked and took off running. We need to wait for the evidence to tell us."

"You can't honestly think Dan did it."

"I'm gathering the evidence. It's up to the prosecutor to charge people."

"But you took him in."

"I did."

"When this all shakes out, you're gonna be painted with the same brush as Spinelli with your overreacting. People up here already hesitate to call you folks because half the time you screw things up worse than if we handled it ourselves."

"Well, sir, we do our best. Appreciate your concern." With that,

Thronson hung up before he lost his temper.

Ed sat staring at the receiver, shaking his head.

~ ~ ~ ~

After leaving the Rockin' A, Spinelli turned left on the main road. He was soon at the Drop-Off and slowed his cruiser as he passed the spot where the shooting occurred. Wally Williams's truck was still there since Dan had not had a chance to retrieve it yet. The county could not arrange for a tow truck to come out this far until tomorrow, so Spinelli decided to stop and have a look. He parked on the far side of the road and walked across.

In the mud that formed since the rain he could see tracks from several vehicles, including the set running through the bushes. There was one leading to Wally's Toyota that was still sitting there, some from Dan's truck where he could see some diesel exhaust soot on the grass, and a pair of dual tires from where the ambulance pulled in. He then found a mystery set from a vehicle that had backed farther into the brush. This one had a passenger car tire tread or all-season tire. When he compared it with the set leading to the Cherokee that was still in the boulders, the Cherokee tires looked a little wider, but the pattern was almost the same. So the rental Cherokee and the other vehicle parked here had similar tires.

So it's likely a rental. Spinelli wrote it in his notes. He searched the area where the mystery car had been parked. The deputy tried to step carefully because it was still a little muddy. When he got to the rear of where the vehicle had been, he spotted something in the grass.

Hmmm, what's this? He bent down and picked up a brass cartridge. Near where he found the brass he spotted a set of unusually large footprints. He placed his foot, which was a size nine, lightly next to the large print and took a picture. Picking up the brass cartridge with a pen from his pocket, he noticed it was a nine millimeter. He scoured the area for more. When he did, he noticed something black that was run over and shoved deep into the mud. He dug it out and saw it was a mirror.

Looks like a left side mirror, he thought as he held it up. He wondered if this could belong to the mystery vehicle that parked there. He crossed over the road and popped the trunk of his patrol car. After taking pictures with his cell phone of their locations, he bagged and tagged the two items he found. He snapped a few more shots, including one that showed the part number on the base of the mirror.

He walked over through the brush to where he could see the Cherokee nose-down in the boulders. The grill of the Jeep was crumpled about a third of the hood length, and it came to rest against a tree on the right side. The left mirror of this vehicle was intact, so the one he found was not from Stevens's car. He walked over to get a look at the passenger side. The right mirror was still there but shoved into the body. He crawled around to see if he could see anything in the Jeep he should retrieve, but it looked like it was cleaned out.

He tried to contain his excitement as he drove the hour into San Jose thinking. Maybe the mirror would help identify what kind of car the shooter was using. Perhaps they could get prints off the cartridge. He was unsure how big Dan's feet were, but between the bullet casing and the shoe prints, it might send the investigation in a new direction. Spinelli was sure Dan didn't do this. He wasn't sure why he had taken a liking to him, but he could tell Dan was a stand-up guy.

Spinelli laughed. *Could be because he has a dog that's smarter than me.*

CHAPTER 16 - SATURDAY EVENING

Being confined was complete torture for Dan. One of the reasons he loved life on the ranch was he could come and go as he pleased. No offices or factory to contain him. He was pacing back and forth in the interrogation room after one of the deputies had mercy on him and unchained him from the table. He received strict instructions to return to his seat whenever anyone came in. But no one had since the interrogation by Thronson and Sanchez two hours ago.

He longed for his whiteboard so he could organize his thoughts better. He also wished he had his phone so he could check on his uncle. Dan wanted to be anywhere but there. He heard a noise at the door and could see Spinelli's face through the small wire-reinforced window in the door. He sat down as the deputy came in.

"How ya doing? You need anything? A Coke?" He sat in the chair opposite Dan.

"A drink sounds great. Coke or Dr. Pepper. Thanks. Is anything happening out there?"

"I think the other two are planning to come back and talk to you some more. I wanted to check on you and to let you know what I found. Thronson hasn't filled me in on anything else yet."

"I appreciate it. Have you found the guy who shot Stevens?"

"Not yet, but I did find some evidence of him." He looked down at Dan's feet. "What shoe size do you wear?"

"Ten and a half." Dan was puzzled by where this was going.

"Do you know what size Ed wears?"

"Nine and a half. Ed tried to give me a pair of boots once, but I couldn't even get them on. Why?"

"I saw some really good-sized footprints out there, near where a mystery vehicle was parked. I also found some brass. I'm hoping we can get some prints off of it."

"You mean a cartridge?"

"Yeah."

"What caliber?"

"Nine millimeter." Spinelli looked proud of himself.

"That's the caliber of my stolen gun. The only prints you'll find on the brass are likely mine."

Spinelli's face visibly sagged along with his shoulders. "Dan, I'm sorry. I was trying to help you and I added nails to your coffin. Shit." He looked totally deflated and fell back in his chair. "What can I do?"

"Maybe the footprints will help. But they may say it was a fireman." Dan looked down at his feet. "What kind of shoes was he wearing?"

"Looked like maybe cowboy boots. Smooth bottoms anyway." He brightened a little. "The firemen probably all wear those big clunkers." The lift helped him remember the mirror. "I also found what looks like a driver's side mirror. I think maybe the agent's car took it off."

"Might be able to at least identify what kind of car we're looking for," Dan said as they both sat up. "Thanks, man."

"I'll go get that drink now. I think Thronson is coming back in to talk to you pretty soon." He stood up and left the room.

Dan sat rocking slightly in his chair, trying to assimilate this new information into his mental storyboard. When he heard the door again, Dan looked up expecting to see Spinelli. Instead, Sanchez and Thronson came in and took their usual positions.

"Mr. Williams, we've done some checking and have a few more questions for you. I want to remind you your answers are being recorded," Sanchez started.

"Okay, shoot." Dan tried not to look as worried as he felt.

"First, we talked to Agent Stevens, and he says he did not resolve things with you and does not remember anything about the conversation you described." Sanchez looked over at Thronson and continued. "He was surprised you left the hospital because he thought he had ordered for you to be taken into custody."

"He was on morphine for Pete's sake. I'd be surprised if he did remember. But what I told you is true." Dan looked pleadingly at Sanchez because he thought Sanchez was still somewhat neutral.

"I'm sure he was on something. His speech was a little slurred, but he sounded reasonably coherent," Sanchez stated matter-of-factly.

"His voice was perfectly fine when he talked to me too initially, but then he started talking crazy." Dan was clinging to hope they would believe him.

"Also, we got back the report on the bullet removed from Agent Stevens. It was a nine millimeter."

Dan's gaze dropped to his hands resting on the table.

"You said the gun that was supposedly stolen from your truck was a nine millimeter?" Sanchez's voice was flat, reviewing things for the tape.

"Yes, sir." Dan tried to sound upbeat and positive.

"And you are aware, I assume, that Deputy Spinelli found some brass in the area where we think the shooting took place?"

"Yes, sir, he mentioned it."

"Yours were the only prints we found on the brass, Mr. Williams." Sanchez sounded more dramatic now.

"I'm not surprised, Detective, since I loaded the gun before it was stolen. I keep that gun under the seat of my truck in case I run into an animal or something. It usually is loaded." Dan was trying not to lose his patience.

"I guess we'll have to file this one under the 'or something' category, huh?" Thronson popped off the wall and leaned on the table.

Dan looked directly at Thronson. "I did not shoot Agent Stevens, or anyone else."

"Okay, okay. Let's move on." Sanchez tried to retake charge of the interview. "Your hands also tested positive for gunpowder."

"Wait. I haven't shot a gun in weeks. That can't be right." Dan stood up, saw the alert reaction of both men and sat down again. "Sorry. That has to be an error."

There was a knock on the glass of the mirror. All three men looked at the mirror. It was Thronson who spoke first.

"Oh, for Pete's sake, Spinelli, I told you to keep your mouth shut if you were going to listen." He exploded from the room.

A few seconds later Dan could hear a muffled conversation in the room behind the mirror. It was getting very animated then stopped abruptly.

Dan asked Sanchez if he could use the restroom. He was escorted to the men's room, Sanchez checked to make sure no one was in it, then let Dan go in. While Dan was standing at the urinal, Spinelli came in carrying a can of Dr. Pepper. He set it on top of the urinal Dan was using and stepped up to the urinal beside him.

"I have to be fast. I told Sanchez I was bringing you the drink and dashed in here before he could tell me to leave it in the conference room."

Dan glanced over, but Spinelli was looking straight ahead, speaking quietly and barely even moving his lips.

"I hate it when they play these mind games. It feels like lying to me. The only place you had gunpowder was on your palms. Probably from touching the rifle Ed handed you."

"Thanks, Spinelli. I was pretty rattled."

"If this went to court, your lawyer could easily pick it apart. They were just using it to scare you." Spinelli glanced toward the door. "And we identified the mirror as coming from a tan Jeep Compass. So we know what to look for now."

"That's great. You're alright, Spinelli." Dan was so relieved to hear some good news he afforded himself the briefest of smiles.

Spinelli broke off and left the room. Dan took his time washing up, to add more cover to Spinelli coming in. Sanchez escorted him back to the interrogation room.

They finally gave Dan a chance to make a call. He phoned Ed and gave him as much of an update as he could in five minutes. Once that was done, he was formally booked and moved downstairs to a cell. Dan always heard about peoples' stomachs dropping when the cell door close. His stomach felt fine, but he would have sworn his heart stopped.

~ ~ ~ ~

Paulo woke up in a cold sweat to the sound of sirens with no idea where he was. He looked around the room, desperately trying to discern his location and an escape route. He got up and peeked through the curtains of the motel room in time to see an ambulance, a local police car and a Highway Patrol car screaming by on the main street outside.

Paulo sat on the bed and tried to control his breathing. His dream was so real he still couldn't believe he was a continent away. He was at his grandfather's ranch, and he was the only grandchild brave enough to go into Opa Erik's library when he was working. Paulo would go and stand quietly at his Opa's side until the man acknowledged him. If he did not look up within a minute or two, Paulo knew he was too busy. However, often he was rewarded with a big smile and a hug. His Opa would sweep him up in his arms and they would go sit near the fireplace in the big leather chair, his grandfather regaling him with stories of the past. Of a fatherland in its glory.

Erik Kraus had been a student, as an undergraduate, of Werner Heisenberg at the University of Berlin, and in Hechingen during the war worked as a low-level "computer" using a slide rule to do the some of the millions of calculations necessary when building a fission

169

device. Erik attended some of Heisenberg's lectures on bomb physics and was so moved that he was ready to follow the man into hell if necessary. Kraus escaped near the end of the war, and being of such little value to the Americans or Russians, had eventually landed in South America. He had met the Argentine ambassador briefly at a party in Berlin and through this casual acquaintance settled in Argentina.

Paulo learned German from his grandfather so he could hear the stories in secret. Opa would talk of untold wealth that had been shipped to South America, which he had helped direct for Martin Bormann, but much of which ended up in the hands of Juan Peron, who was coming into power at that time. There had always been rumors of subs that had sunk off the coast, but no one could find them. Sunken treasure that was rightfully theirs.

Opa married an Argentine woman who was very traditional Catholic but had been educated in the United States. His grandmother believed his grandfather's work had failed not because of Hitler, but because they had gotten too close to the face of God. She quoted the Bible and Exodus: "You cannot see my face, for no man can see the face of God and live." Regardless, she taught Paulo Spanish and English, which served him well in his studies. He majored in physics to impress his grandfather but was not able to rise to the level he hoped. His last chance he felt was to try to recover some of what was stolen by the Americans after the war.

In his dream, Paulo went up to his Opa, who was working feverishly on some calculations at his desk. He could not get his grandfather's attention, so he began to tap him on the shoulder. Suddenly, without even looking up, his grandfather raised one arm and pointed to a door Paulo never noticed before in the den. Paulo approached it cautiously, seeing a casket. He stepped into the room, but as his adult self, and was drawn to it.

Approaching the coffin, he recognized his Opa Erik lying there in repose. In his mind, Paulo implored his grandfather to forgive him for his failures in his academic accomplishments. Standing beside the coffin, he looked down at his grandfather's face. Tears were streaming down Paulo's cheeks when suddenly his grandfather opened his eyes, looked directly at Paulo and shook his head in disappointment. He closed his eyes, never to smile on Paulo again.

Paulo sat on the edge of the bed wiping his face. He thought of the disasters that plagued him this week and vowed to make things right by finding the binder and folder he saw the old man take. Paulo would commit his life to recovering Opa's fortune. At least he had Willis's notebook, but it was critical to get the other papers.

His grandfather had talked about quantum physics and how in some dimension of the universe they succeeded in making the bomb and Germany ruled supreme. In yet another, all of the leaders had escaped to Argentina with their spoils of war and had begun anew. Paulo believed a fortune in gold could be the key to a more glorious future.

He showered and dressed to go. Walking across the street to the grocery store he bought some meat, cheese, and bread, which he stuffed into his backpack. He would ride up to the ranch and eat while he waited for his chance to strike. Climbing on the bike, he strapped on the pack and headed up Mines Road in his anonymous helmet. On his other trips on the remote drive he only saw a few vehicles, and those were mostly four-wheel-drive trucks and SUVs. Today he saw two police cars from the highway patrol before he was halfway. He was not aware there was a motorcycle accident earlier in the day and that the patrol cars were returning from taking care of that.

When he saw Ed approaching, he recognized the truck and driver as belonging to the ranch. Maybe the older man had the binders with him. Paulo decided to follow the rancher. He pulled to the side of the road and tried to look casual. Just a guy admiring the view. Once the truck passed, he turned around and followed at a distance. He would at least check the old man's vehicle to see if the files were in it. If not, perhaps the rancher would lead him to them.

⬚

~ ~ ~ ~

Ed had a hunch that he decided to pursue. He was familiar enough with the Life Flight operation that he hoped there would be some evidence of what was said by the agent on the flight. Ed called the company but could get no one who would give him any information. So he drove to the CDF fire station to see if he could talk to the captain. As he pulled up, O'Shea was walking to the office from the garage that held the trucks.

"Hello. Mr. Wyath, is it? What can I do for you?" O'Shea extended his hand to Ed.

"Please, call me Ed." He smiled and shook hands with the captain.

"I was driving by and wanted to thank you guys for all the hard work lately. If you're not saving our ranches from burning to the ground, you're patching us up when we get hurt. I wanted you guys to know it's appreciated."

O'Shea smiled and motioned him into the office. He spoke as they were taking a seat. "Why thank you, Ed. It's what we get paid to do, but it's nice to know folks notice once in a while. Can I get you some coffee?"

"I wouldn't say no to a cup."

The captain poured two mugs full of coffee and placed one in front of Ed. He set a plastic container on the desk containing packets of powdered cream and sugar.

Ed helped himself to some creamer, using a plastic stirrer to mix it. "Looks like the rain ought to keep things from being too dry this year."

"It's good to get some rain in May for a change. The last few years have been pretty dry and kept us busy during the fire season."

This wasn't idle small talk about the weather. Both men's livelihood was directly impacted by rainfall each year. They chatted about past fire seasons for a while. The Rockin' A had been hit by a few fires over the years. Ed shared some old stories about some of the senior CDF managers he'd encountered as he helped them fight fires by creating firebreaks with the small bulldozer he kept on the ranch. O'Shea was in stitches with one story about a now senior manager who Ed had to rescue on his property because the fireman was lost in the hills.

"I hear there's another major storm coming in tomorrow. Just heard it on the scanner." O'Shea motioned toward a scanner in the corner that squawked occasionally. "Radio was saying to batten down the hatches for this one."

"Too much is almost as bad as not enough." Ed thought about all the work he'd have to do to get ready for a major storm. Making sure the animals were all okay and equipment was protected, not to mention both the roof on the barn and the storage sheds were getting up in age.

Ed decided to pass on the second cup of coffee and said he better get going. As he was headed out the door, he turned around. "I wanted to apologize if your crew got spooked the other day when they came upon Dan with a rifle. I gave it to him after finding that guy shot. I didn't want to leave them there unprotected." He was relieved when the captain smiled.

"It did give them pause for a second to be called out to a gunshot wound and come up on a guy with a rifle sitting there. But they were fine." He patted Ed on the shoulder. "We are required to report it to

173

the sheriff, though."

Ed nodded. "Do you know who was on the Life Flight crew that transported the guy who was shot? I wanted to thank them too."

O'Shea thought for a second. "I'm not sure, but I could find out."

"Don't go to too much trouble. I wanted to ask the guys a question or two." Ed didn't want to push too hard.

"About what?"

"Well, during the flight my nephew said he and the agent settled things, but after his surgery the agent didn't remember and thought he left without authorization. Do you know if they record the voices on the flight?" Ed watched the captain's face to see if he touched a sensitive area, but O'Shea showed no reaction.

"I know they record the crew, in case there's a problem on the flight. Typical flight recorder stuff." He paused. "And I am pretty sure they record everybody, for medical liability reasons."

Ed grinned. "God bless American lawyers."

"Exactly. I know those guys pretty well, and I might be able to get them to send me the audio file."

"Really?" Ed didn't imagine it would be so easy.

"Sure. Since we radio back and forth with the flight crew, my guys are on the recordings also, so they provide us with feedback on the exchanges occasionally to improve the processes." O'Shea's brow wrinkled as he struggled to remember. "I think I handled that exchange and I can't remember if I told the crew your nephew was under arrest, just that he was accompanying the patient. I'm curious myself now."

The captain picked up the phone, and after being transferred three times finally ended up talking to the guy who collected all the recordings for storage at a central site. He told O'Shea that they retain them for seven years, so everything is digitized and saved on a server. O'Shea gave him an incident number, thanked him and hung up the phone.

"Now we wait," O'Shea said. "Sure you don't want another cup?"

"How long do we wait?"

"Not long." He pointed to the computer screen on his desk. It showed his email inbox. "But it might take a few minutes to download a file that size."

"You talked me into it." Ed picked up his cup off the desk and went over to help himself.

Twenty minutes later the email arrived and the file finally downloaded. Upon review, O'Shea confirmed that he said nothing to the flight crew about Dan being under arrest. When they listened to the conversation between Stevens and Dan, they were dumbfounded.

"I'm not sure I can let you have the file now. That sounds like pretty high-level stuff," O'Shea said. "I'm not even cleared to hear most of it."

"I plan to go straight to Agent Stevens from here and hand it to him, to see if he remembers it." Ed gave a quick nod to emphasize his point. "You're welcome to come along. The more people he knows have heard this, the less like it is to be swept under a rug."

O'Shea sat and thought for a minute before answering. "You know, my shift is ending and it would be nice to follow up with a patient for a change. I generally never find out how they did." He smiled at Ed and winked. After downloading the file to a thumb drive and packing up his laptop, he went in the back to inform his crew he was leaving.

Both men jumped into Ed's truck and headed in the direction of Livermore on the way to the hospital in Castro Valley. About halfway to town, they saw a tall guy with a dirt bike. Ed started to stop and see if he needed help, but as they came closer the rider threw his leg over it and Ed could hear it start. Ed saw him pull out behind them, but he stayed back instead of blasting past like most of the bikers do on that road.

~ ~ ~ ~

Thronson was so hot after Spinelli knocked on the window that the deputy decided to make himself scarce. Wally Williams had been transferred to the Santa Clara County Medical Center, where there was a new department for brain injuries, and Spinelli decided to stop in and see if he was starting to remember anything else. On the way to the hospital, the announcer on the news radio station talked about a massive storm bearing down on the Bay Area. Storms meant car accidents for the deputy.

He arrived at the hospital and checked with the nurses' station to make sure Wally could receive visitors.

"Sure. I think the patient has a couple of people in there with him now." The nurse pointed down the hallway to the room.

As Spinelli approached the door, he could hear Wally's voice.

"I was jumped by three guys, and the worst of it is that they jumped me from behind. Cowards."

It sounded like he was pretty animated. Spinelli assumed it was from whatever drugs they were giving him. As he turned the corner, he could see two men standing next to the bed. He recognized them as Bud and Harvey, the two local characters who were at the scene on the day of the murder. Bud was the one who identified the hammer as belonging to Dan.

"Three of 'em, huh?" Harvey said. Both men were shaking their heads.

"At least. It would take that many to hog-tie me that way." Wally laughed. "I'm kind of a big deal you know."

"How do you know there were three of them if they knocked you out from behind?" Spinelli interrupted the storytelling.

"Hey, Speedy. What are you doing here? Did ya get locked in your trunk again?" Wally was talking faster and louder than usual, so he was definitely on something.

"No." Spinelli looked down and shook his head. "I'm just checking on you to see how you're doing." He looked up and smiled at Wally. "So how do you know there were three of them?"

"Because when I was tied up and blindfolded they asked me questions. When I wouldn't answer them in English, they tried German and Spanish." He held up the hand without an IV drip in it and counted off the languages on his fingers as he spoke. "The one that spoke English tried first, and when I didn't answer the other two jumped in."

"I didn't know you spoke German or Spanish, Wally." Harvey looked impressed.

"I don't, but I've heard 'em enough to recognize the gibberish."

"You're sure those were the languages?" Spinelli took out his notebook and started writing.

"Pretty much. There were definitely three different ones I could tell." Wally poked his finger in the air at Spinelli to make his point.

"Is anything else coming back to you?"

"Nah, it's all pretty fuzzy." Wally frowned. "But I'm sure about the three languages."

~ ~ ~ ~

Ed and Captain O'Shea arrived at Eden Medical Center in Castro Valley a little after five. When Ed asked about Wally, they said he was transferred to Santa Clara because of his head injury. That would not be good for his wife, Bobbie, who would have to drive all the way from Modesto to visit. For security reasons because of the gunshot wound, they would not tell him Agent Stevens's room number. However, when Captain O'Shea stepped up and showed his ID, they provided it immediately.

"You're coming in pretty handy today." Ed poked him with an elbow as they left the nurses' station.

"I'll try not to make a habit of it," O'Shea joked.

There was a local policeman outside when they approached the room, and the captain's ID saved them again. Inside was another man in a suit, who quickly stood up when they approached. Once he identified who they were, he relaxed and asked them how long they would be visiting. He talked to Agent Stevens a second then told them he'd go grab something from the cafeteria. They assured him they would look after the agent. The man in the suit talked to the policeman outside the door then walked down the hall.

Agent Stevens was a little more alert than he had been in the previous twenty-four hours. He insisted the staff take him off of the morphine. The agent looked to be in a bit of pain, but his speech was less slurred. He did not know either of the gentlemen who entered the room, but when he heard them introduce themselves he was curious.

"What can I do for you gentlemen, or did you just stop in to check up on me?" He looked from Ed to Captain O'Shea.

They looked at each other and Ed began. "Agent Stevens, my nephew, Dan Williams, and I found you the other night. We arrived together. He went with you on the helicopter flight to bring your equipment, and he said you worked everything out."

"Well, that was before I knew he stole federal property. And I don't remember discussing anything about the case with him. If he hadn't already been in the custody of the sheriff, I would have him arrested. He interfered with a federal investigation." His pain was putting him in a foul mood, and he had little patience for this.

"So you don't remember talking to Dan on the flight?" Ed asked.

"No, I do not."

Ed looked at O'Shea again. "Well, we have a recording of it from the helicopter communication system. Would you like to hear it?"

Stevens was now wary of having been set up. "Okay."

O'Shea produced a small laptop out of the briefcase he carried and inserted the thumb drive containing the audio file. The recording began playing. When Stevens heard himself slurring about 'screwing with the DOE' the agent cringed. By the time they were discussing the Nazi Bell and gold shipments, he was white as the sheet on the bed and sputtering.

"You're not cleared to hear this." He was reaching for the laptop. "I have to confiscate that."

"Now hold on there." Ed pulled the laptop out of reach. "This file is already part of the public record that I can get my hands on regarding my nephew's treatment during the flight."

Stevens looked like he was going to blow a fuse. However, when it got to the part where he was describing the guy who shot him, he sat up. "That's right. It's coming back now." Listening to his own voice giving a description of the tall man triggered memories.

"So this clears Dan of anything to do with shooting you?"

"Of course."

"And you said you would forgive taking the cameras if he returned the files."

"I won't bring any federal charges if he gets them to me immediately." He was hedging about the local charges, trying to keep them as his backup.

"Will you work with the sheriff to get any other charges dropped?" Ed was going for broke.

"Why should I do that? It's out of my hands."

"Well..." Ed gestured toward the laptop.

"Are you threatening a federal agent with blackmail, Mr. Wyath?"

"I wouldn't dream of such a thing." Ed put on his best 'oh gosh-darn country boy face' and shrugged. "But if a dumb rancher like me could figure out that such information existed on the public record, I would hate to think what a big city lawyer would come up with if

Dan had to hire one."

"Okay, Mr. Wyath, you win."

With that, O'Shea pulled out the thumb drive and handed it to Stevens. Both he and Ed put their index fingers to their lips indicating they would tell no one.

The other agent walked in from the cafeteria, so they spun on their heels and walked out.

As they were heading across the parking lot to Ed's truck, O'Shea spoke. "Remind me not to do any horse trading with you, will you?"

Ed smiled and kept walking.

When they got to his truck, Ed threw his reading glasses and case in the console. He noticed that it looked as if a few things were out of place. But with nothing missing, Ed dismissed it as Dan or Margaret having searched for something. He was too happy with his and O'Shea's small victory to worry about it.

CHAPTER 17 - SUNDAY, MAY 16TH

Dan had never spent a night in jail before. He woke up Sunday morning after a fitful sleep. He was trapped in a cage and not able to do a single thing to help himself. If he was convicted and sent to prison, he was sure he would lose his mind. The breakfast they served made airline food look good.

He'd talked to Ed yesterday evening but heard nothing regarding whether any progress was being made. He hoped Ed was arranging for a decent lawyer. He did know Wally had been taken to a hospital in Santa Clara specializing in head trauma and wondered if that meant it was something serious.

How could things have gone this wrong so fast? He was usually the one who went around and fixed things, and now he was helpless in a cell. Maybe he shouldn't have talked to Thronson and Sanchez at all. Everything he told them, they twisted and turned back on him. If Spinelli hadn't warned him in the restroom about the gunpowder residue, he would have been even more panic-stricken. He was glad Janet was not still alive to see him in here. The thought of his dead wife was all it took for him to start sobbing into his bunk. After a few minutes, he stopped and sat up. He would not feel sorry for himself. He would turn that into anger. The anger would motivate him to fight. The key was to find the SOB behind all this and to trust the ones he loved to come to his aid.

~ ~ ~ ~

Sunday was supposed to be his day off, but that was ruined by a message from a frantic Agent Stevens, who insisted on a conference call at 9:00 a.m. Thronson was up, dressed and in the office by eight-thirty. If he had to work, he might as well go in. Thronson called both Sanchez and Spinelli to tell them to join the call from home. Maybe he would be able to leave by noon and salvage part of the day. It didn't matter because rain was already coming down pretty steady and they were predicting a record-breaking storm. During the last few years, the weather was like a toggle switch. It would either be bone dry or it would turn torrential.

He was on his second cup of coffee and had already eaten a bagel he brought for breakfast by the time the call needed to start. He logged on early to the conference line since he was supposed to host it. As soon as he put in the code to activate the conference, the announcement said there were two parties connected.

"Who's on the line?" Thronson was a bit annoyed he had to start immediately. He joined five minutes early to give him time to collect his thoughts and focus.

"This is Deputy Spinelli. Is that you, Lieutenant?"

"Yes. Good morning."

"Good morning, sir. I've got some new information." Spinelli was anxious to share what he learned about the multiple perpetrators in the abduction of Wally Williams.

"Why don't we wait for the others so we don't have to repeat things?" Maybe he could still get a minute or two of peace.

"Okay."

Spinelli poured himself some coffee from the pot he just brewed. He sat in his living room and looked out the window at the relentless rain.

"No problem with working today, sir. With this weather, I expect to be called in eventually. There's bound to be a slew of accidents."

So much for his peaceful thoughts. "Yes, it's likely. They are predicting quite a storm."

Sanchez joined the call, with the sound of children in the background. To keep Spinelli from rattling on about things, Thronson decided to share something he had learned. First, he double-checked to see if Stevens had joined yet.

"Agent Stevens? You on here?" No answer.

"I haven't heard him," Spinelli finally responded.

"Good. I wanted to let you know what I've learned about Agent Stevens from a good friend at the FBI," Thronson began. "Seems he's a CIA wannabe. Apparently, he flunked out because he was highly susceptible to interrogation using drugs. Rumor has it in the Bureau that if you give the guy an aspirin, he'll give you his social security number." Thronson laughed. "That must be why he's such a prick about throwing his federal status around."

Sanchez chuckled.

Finally, five minutes late, Stevens dialed in. "Gentlemen, what's the latest we have on the Willis incident?" No apologies or good morning.

Thronson hated how the feds always thought their time was more valuable. He was determined to take control of this meeting. "How about we start with what we've learned about the shooting and then work back. Detective, tell him what we've know." They were his people, and he was setting the agenda, by God.

Sanchez jumped in. "Sure. The bullet was a nine millimeter, which is consistent with the gun Williams claims was stolen from his truck. We don't have the gun yet, so we can't prove it was his." He paused, but no one jumped in. "Deputy Spinelli went back to the scene of the shooting and did find brass, with Williams's prints on them."

"Williams is not your guy," Stevens said with little enthusiasm. "He didn't shoot me."

"How do you know? You said you didn't remember." Thronson

183

was pissed. After all the work to build this case against Williams, now Stevens was blowing it out of the water.

"It's started to come back to me." He was stretching the truth a bit, but these yokels didn't need to know. "The shooter was much taller than Williams. I got a glancing look at him."

"Did you see his car?" Spinelli asked.

"I seem to remember he was standing behind a light-colored SUV."

"Do you know if you grazed the side of it?" Spinelli was thinking of the mirror he found.

"No idea. I saw my windshield explode and felt the pain. All I wanted to do was get out of there, so I floored it."

"Well, we found a driver's side mirror off a tan Jeep Compass at the scene. We know it was tan because one of the bolts sheared off a piece of the doorframe," Spinelli added.

"Could be. Sounds about right."

"Where was the shooter relative to the Jeep? Was he behind it about three feet?" That's where Spinelli found the footprints.

"He was behind it, but I have no idea how far."

"Deputy, we haven't confirmed yet it was a Jeep, so stop jumping to conclusions," Thronson corrected. He turned his attention to Stevens. "So you're saying Williams is not your shooter?"

"Definitely not. You can't charge him with that." The agent thought about the recording again and how it could end his career.

"Dammit!" Thronson exploded before he could control his temper. "Okay, so we drop those charges, but we still have him on interfering with an investigation and possibly being involved in the Willis killing either directly or after the fact."

"Well, Lieutenant, about that..." Stevens was trying to think of how to approach this.

"Oh, for Pete's sake. Are you saying we need to cut him loose entirely?" Thronson wanted to scream.

"I remember now that I grilled him a little on the helicopter ride. He hoped Willis had put the cameras in and that the killer would be caught on the recordings. They were outside of the crime scene, so it'd be a stretch to claim interference."

"But he went into the building. It's on the tapes."

Sanchez cringed when he heard Thronson say this.

"Lieutenant, how could you know that? You don't have a copy of the files. Those are federal property, and if you made a copy, you're as guilty as Williams." It felt good to Stevens to retake the offensive.

Thronson backpedaled as fast as he could. "I'll turn them over to you immediately. You were, uh, incapacitated."

"You can't use any part of those tapes against Williams or his uncle. And the fact that you lied to my face when you turned over the equipment will be noted in my report." Stevens started to really enjoy this.

"So we have nothing on Williams?" Sanchez tried to divert the group.

"Not unless you've come up with new evidence." Stevens decided to let the diversion work for now.

Sanchez wanted to push forward. "Let's move on to the kidnapping of Wally Williams."

Spinelli jumped in, anxious. "I have some new information on that."

"Go ahead."

"I did some checking on the secret room. I talked to Willis's wife about it. She said he built it as a bomb shelter back in the 1950s, and then started using it as a private place to work. Said he used to work in the house but her vacuuming all the time drove him crazy."

"Sounds like the cranky old bastard," Thronson interjected.

"I stopped by the hospital in Santa Clara yesterday to interview Wally Williams again. Anyway, he was telling his friends there were three guys," Spinelli added.

"Three?" Stevens was confused.

"Yes. Wally said when he was questioned about the files he took, they spoke to him in English, German, and Spanish."

"Did he see three guys?" Stevens asked.

"No, they had him blindfolded, but at different times they tried questions in all three." Spinelli was searching his notes to see if he had written anything else.

"Could he tell if the voices were different, or did one person speak all three?"

"I didn't ask him that." Spinelli was kicking himself mentally for not thinking of it.

"Thank you, Detective Spinelli. That could be critical information." Stevens was frantically writing notes now.

"It's deputy, sir, and you're welcome." Spinelli hoped Thronson would notice the mistake.

Sanchez wanted to wrap things up so he could get back to his family. "Was there anything else we needed to cover?"

Everyone said no. Thronson was in such a foul mood he was barely listening. "Okay, so sounds like we cut Williams loose on all charges. Do we go after his uncle for removing evidence?"

Stevens jumped in first. "No. If he hadn't removed it, we would have lost it. So he ended up doing us a favor. I think a slap on the wrist will suffice. They have promised to bring it to me immediately."

"So we're back to square one?" Now Thronson was feeling sick. His boss would not be happy.

"No. I have some ideas based on what Detective Spinelli found. You should hear from me as soon as I check a few things. Thanks, gentlemen." Stevens hung up before they could answer.

Sanchez spoke up. "Hey, Spinelli. Maybe you should go work for the DOE. You could be a detective over there."

"Don't go getting a big head, Spinelli." With that, Thronson hung up.

~ ~ ~ ~

Dan was annoyed at first when he saw Spinelli and how happy he seemed. How could anyone be so chipper when his whole world was falling apart? As soon as he thought it, he slapped himself mentally for being so self-centered. Spinelli came whistling into the holding cell area where Dan was housed. When he opened the door, Dan assumed he was going to the interrogation room.

"What the heck has gotten into you, Spinelli? Did you get lucky last night or something?"

"Nope." He guided Dan down the hallway.

"Must be this spring weather we're having," Dan joked.

"It's raining buckets right now. Supposed to get worse." Spinelli was having fun because it wasn't often he could have the advantage over Dan.

"I'm surprised you're even here on a Sunday. Don't they give you any days off?" Dan was beginning to wonder where they were going. They turned down toward the offices where he was processed instead of going upstairs to the detectives' offices.

"I was supposed to be off, but I came in to take care of a couple things. It's a lousy day out anyway."

"Where are you taking me, to the torture rack?" He wondered who would be questioning him on a Sunday.

"I'm not taking you anywhere. You've been sprung. All the charges have been dropped." He watched Dan's face as it sank in.

"Spinelli, don't you joke with me. I just spent my first night in lockup, and I will slap you silly." He stood waiting for the punch line.

"After I came in on a Sunday to process you out? I could've made you wait until tomorrow, pal."

"Wait. You're serious?"

Spinelli smiled and nodded. Dan reached down and picked up the shorter deputy and grasped him in a bear hug.

"Thank you, Speedy."

Two deputies who were walking down the hall reacted by turning toward them and putting their hands on their pistols, not sure if Dan was assaulting a fellow deputy.

"Put me down, you moron." Spinelli stepped back and adjusted his belt, scolding the ecstatic ex-prisoner.

The other officers relaxed and snickered. One of them said in a mock stage voice, "Did he say Speedy or Sweetie?"

Spinelli turned beet red.

Spinelli finished processing Dan out, avoiding any further physical contact other than a handshake when they got to the door. Earlier, Spinelli had called Ed to arrange for him to come and get Dan. Dan did not care about the pouring rain as he walked outside. He spread his arms, looked up and breathed in the air of freedom. Ed sat in his truck watching the crazy man twirling around in the rain. He was soaked by the time he climbed into the passenger's seat.

"You're getting my seats wet." Ed reached behind his seat and grabbed a towel from the back seat. "I thought we'd go see Wally while we're down here. They moved him to Santa Clara Valley Medical."

"Let's go. Anywhere but here."

"You hungry? Wanna grab a sandwich on the way?" Ed pulled away from the curb and into the downpour.

"Sounds great. Thanks for picking me up again."

"Spinelli said it sounds like they've got you in the clear now, so hopefully this is the last time." Ed didn't mention his role in getting Dan released.

"God, I hope so." Dan felt himself tearing up, but he wasn't sure if it was happiness or fear of being brought back there that was doing it. He quickly recovered. "Did he tell you anything else?"

"Just that Wally may have helped them break the case. Something about three guys holding him captive." Ed tried to concentrate on the drive because the streets were beginning to flood in places.

"Three of them?" Dan wondered aloud.

~ ~ ~ ~

About the time Ed and Dan were pulling away, Thronson's phone rang.

"Thronson," he answered. It was Stevens on the line. Thronson never had a fed return his call this soon.

"Lieutenant, I wanted to get back to you. The three languages triggered something for me. I had some of my guys check it out, and it might've paid off."

Why do the feds always have guys? Thronson pictured each agent having dozens of minions running around the federal buildings checking and double-checking each angle of every clue. He had trouble getting paperclips. "What've you got?" was all he responded.

"We checked with TSA, and there was a guy we've been tracking from Argentina who entered the country early this week. He's the grandson of a Nazis who immigrated to South America after the war."

"Really?"

"Yes, and get this. The guy rented a bright yellow Chevy Camaro." Thronson wondered where he was going with this.

"Then he swapped it for a tan Jeep Compass a day later in Livermore."

"No kidding? You have a location?" Now Thronson was interested. Maybe Stevens did have a clue.

"Nothing on the credit cards but the exchange of the cars was done at a motel in Livermore. We're checking it out now. He may've been paying cash for the motel."

"That's Alameda County, out of my jurisdiction, but let me know if I can help in any way."

"Will do. FBI is also assisting. I'll keep you informed." Stevens started to hang up but heard Thronson talking, so put the phone back to his ear.

"Oh, FYI. We turned Williams loose."

"It's the right thing to do. Thanks." Stevens hung up and stole a look at the thumb drive still in his laptop. He had turned his hospital room into a command post, but now he needed to get out of there. Things were starting to move fast.

Thronson called Sanchez and Spinelli to fill them in.

"It was your tip about the three languages that clued him in, Spinelli. No wonder you're his hero." He could almost hear Spinelli's head swell over the phone but gave him his moment. "Nice job."

"Is there anything you want me to do to help, sir?" Spinelli wanted to keep the pursuit up on their end.

"Maybe we should post some men at the edge of the county on the southern route out of there to keep an eye out for the Compass," Sanchez suggested. "The road toward Patterson comes out in Stanislaus County, and the Livermore side is Alameda. That's why Stevens called in the FBI. Do we have any photos of the guy?"

"Good idea, Sanchez. Let's get Stevens to send us a description and pictures if he has them. Can you set that up?"

"No problem."

"Keep me posted." Thronson hung up.

~ ~ ~ ~

Paulo was finally feeling rested after a night in a real bed at the motel. He walked across the street and enjoyed an American breakfast at a chain restaurant. After going back to his room to pick up the motorcycle helmet and the pistol, he climbed on and started the bike. It was going to be an uncomfortable ride with the rain coming down. The jacket helped a little, but since the sleeves were too short his wrists and lower arms started getting wet so he was cold as he rode up Mines Road. The brisk temperatures helped him stay awake at least.

The ride was a bit surreal as he climbed the winding road up into the low-hanging storm clouds. They were a mixture of steel gray and black in color, and the wind was pushing them with the fast-moving storm. He would occasionally break out of the fog as he dipped down into small valleys, but would soon climb back up into the gray mass of clouds, causing his face shield to fog. The closeness of the mist and clouds, combined with the dim light, made it hard to judge where he was on the road and made the trip seem much longer than usual. He almost lost control when a cattle guard suddenly appeared in the mist. The metal grates that prevent cows from crossing were slippery in the wet conditions, causing the bike's rear tire to kick out to the side.

The good news was there was almost no activity on the road. Paulo doubted if the deputies and the CHP would want to be out in this weather searching through the woods. He would have the advantage and should be able to accomplish his mission, then get out of the area. With this weather, his first objective was to return the motorcycle and retrieve his car to get out of this rain. When he passed Sam's Place, there were only a few older pickups sitting in the parking lot, and he could barely make out the neon beer signs in the window.

At the ranch where he stole the truck, Paulo could see a woman loading some horses into a trailer, so he decided to wait until after dark to search the shop. When he slowed the bike to get a better look, one of the dogs beside the trailer turned and looked at him. It began to bark ferociously and shot up the hill toward the road. Paulo gunned the motorcycle and took off. It was raining too hard to see clearly in the small mirror of the dirt bike, but when he turned his head back to check the dog had stopped in the middle of the road, staring at him as he raced away.

When he finally reached the cabin, he was chilled to the bone. Fortunately, no one was around. It must only be used occasionally for hunting. There was a small wood stove, so Paulo decided to start a fire to dry off and warm himself. He stripped to his underwear and sat in a chair by the stove wrapped in a blanket he pulled off the bed. Paulo would make one more attempt to search the old man's secret room and then deal with his captive if the old man was still alive.

Warmed by the fire and the blanket, he fell asleep.

CHAPTER 18 - SUNDAY AFTERNOON

When Dan and Ed entered Wally's hospital room, he was sitting on the edge of the bed and was dressed. His wife Bobbie was there, and a small duffle bag was packed with his things.

Wally smiled at them as they came in. "I'm breaking out of this joint."

"You mean we came all the way down here to see you and you're not even sick?" Ed joked. He turned to Dan. "Boy. Some people." He broke into a big smile and patted Wally on the back. "Glad to see you up and around, Wally. How's the head?"

Dan hugged his uncle and aunt.

"Well, they did X-rays and CAT scans and every test they could think of and still didn't find any brains. I tried to tell them."

Bobbie shook her head. "He has a severe concussion but he should be okay, they said. He has to take it easy for a while, so I'm clipping his wings for the next week or two."

"Hey, I heard you broke the case for the cops." Dan finally managed to get a word in.

"I did? Nobody told me." Wally looked around at each of them. "Damn, I'm good."

"That thing you told them about the three languages registered something for Agent Stevens," Ed explained. "It pointed to somebody they were watching, I guess."

"That must be why they let me go." Dan still wasn't sure how he had been cleared of everything.

"You mean to tell me you didn't bust out?" Wally said as he looked at his nephew disapprovingly.

"No. Speedy came and sprung me this morning. I don't care how I got out, I'm just happy I am." He gave his uncle a serious look.

"You really think there were three guys?"

"I'm still a little fuzzy on it, but I know I got asked questions in three languages. I guess the guys, or guy, assumed I could speak German since I took those papers. Besides, it would take that many to bring a tough guy like me down." Wally winked at him.

Bobbie rolled her eyes.

"Heck, Uncle, Syd could take you down."

"Of course Syd could, that's the smartest dog in the world."

At that point, a nurse came in with a wheelchair and the release papers. They filed out of the room and headed home.

When Ed pulled into the ranch and Dan stepped out of the passenger side, Syd was about thirty yards away. She saw Dan and shot across the yard like a furry streak of lightning, leaping and hitting him at chest height with her front paws. Both went tumbling backward into the mud at the edge of the carport where Dan stood. Syd let out a high-pitched bark and started licking Dan's face, and Dan lay there laughing.

"Now you're going to need to strip and get a shower before Margaret lets you in the house," Ed said as he shook his head and smiled at the display of affection.

Dan laughed and got up. He stood outside and stripped to his underwear and carried his clothes inside to the washer. Thirty minutes later they were sitting at the kitchen table, Dan wearing some old sweats of Ed's, talking about the events of the past few days. Dan almost teared up again when he realized that sitting around this table with them was the real representation of home to him. He felt safe, warm, dry and relaxed for the first time in three days.

Dan spent the rest of the afternoon helping Ed and Margaret check the animals on both portions of the ranch. The weather was getting worse, and they wanted to ensure none of the cattle would be caught in a low-lying area. After dinner, Dan decided he'd better get back to the shop and make some progress on some of the projects that were behind schedule.

~ ~ ~ ~

Spinelli was sitting at the entrance to the parking lot at Joseph Grant Park watching County Road 130 going up to Mt. Hamilton. The spot gave him a clear view of any cars coming down the mountain for several miles. The terrain became rolling hills at this point, so the road was much more visible. He would be able to see the tan Jeep Compass in plenty of time to radio it in and set up a roadblock. He coordinated with Alameda County and the CHP to cover the other two roads leading out of the hills.

He heard via the police radio that the raid on the motel was a bust. Well, not completely. They found the guy's room and his luggage, but Paulo Kraus was not there. The good news was they confirmed he was in the area. They knew what type of vehicle he was driving, and now they had a name, description, and picture. The trap was set at all the exits of the hills, so it should be a matter of time.

Agent Stevens had not shared all of the details, so Spinelli found himself wondering what in the world a criminal from South America would be doing up in the hills above San Jose. He knew there were occasional busts of illegal pot operations in the remote sections. Maybe one of the drug cartels was trying to move into the area. He wasn't sure how Willis got mixed up with them, or if it was even related to the Willis murder, but he knew this Kraus shot a federal agent.

Spinelli was glad he was able to help a bit in clearing Dan's name. You never know what will be a break in a case like this. He sat in his patrol car sipping coffee from his thermos and daydreaming about actually being called detective someday.

The rain was becoming torrential, and it was getting tough to see very far up the road. Spinelli moved a little closer to the edge of the highway and turned on the defroster and wipers as darkness began to fall. He was determined not to let the tan Jeep Compass get past him. Things were starting to happen quickly now, though it didn't seem like it sitting on a stakeout.□

CHAPTER 19 - SUNDAY EVENING

It felt better to turn his mind off and get into the rhythm of doing some physical work. Dan had already done the calculations and sketched out everything, only needing to follow his own instructions. He began cutting metal to length, machining, and welding.

When Dan wasn't making noise, he would stop to listen to the sound of the hard rain on the metal roof of the shop. This is where he belonged. It satisfied both his creative side and the physical reward of building things and gave him a tremendous feeling of accomplishment. Syd curled up on her bed in the corner while Dan happily plowed through his work. He was precise and meticulous in his planning and execution. If his name was associated with it, it was going to be done correctly.

It was hard to tell how long he had worked. When he looked outside, it was getting dark. He walked over and closed the roll-up door a little and noticed the storyboard he and Wally started the other day. Absentmindedly, he added information learned since they last touched it. Wally's abduction, his truck theft, and the agent's shooting were the first items added to index cards and taped up. He included the tan Compass and the little bit of information he knew about the guy they were looking for. The suspect was tall, wore size thirteen shoes and had Dan's gun. Off to the side, he cryptically wrote down the information learned from the agent during the flight. He substituted agency for DEA and German instead of Nazi. He added war expert next to Willis's name, along with tracking subs and the word watched. Near the suspect he jotted languages and the letters E, G, and S.

He stepped back to get a broader perspective and think a bit. It was definitely some pretty heavy stuff, and he still wasn't sure how much he even believed. He pulled out his smartphone to record his notes as a video and scanned the wall in front of him, making a few verbal comments about what each meant. As he was finishing, he heard a noise outside and, being distracted, lay the phone face down on a table with the camera still running as he turned to investigate the noise.

Dan hit the button to roll the door up enough for him to duck under and get a look outside. Before his eyes could adjust to the twilight, he felt a stream of water hit his boots. The noise he'd heard was the trickling sound of water as it ran down the hill directly toward his shop. The tracks his truck made when the guy who stole it drove it up the incline caused three problems. First, the tire tracks created two large ruts that now turned into small ditches pointed straight at the door of the shop. Second, at the top, the tires had cut through the berm running along the road that keeps the water from cascading down the side. With the damage it did, all of the water draining off of the asphalt was now pouring straight down the hill. And finally, the tracks at the bottom where the truck had turned to go up created a small dam, trapping the water temporarily and resulting in a pond.

What he'd heard was the water as it finally reached the top of the berm and began trickling into his shop. As Dan stood there, the dam seemed to burst and the water poured over the tire tracks. The gushing stream carried enough mud that it quickly plugged the one drain placed in front of the door to prevent water from coming inside. With the blockage and the water rising, the small lake now headed into the shop.

Dan spun around and looked at the floor, now with an inch of water on it, and noticed all the electrical cords running across it. Syd got up from her bed, which was getting wet, and came over to investigate what Dan was doing. Concerned for Syd's safety, Dan called her, waded out to his truck, and opened the door.

"Mount up, Syd," he said as he put her in the cab where she would be safe. With Syd taken care of, he returned to the shop then began unplugging things and making sure all the power tools were off the floor and on the tables. He paid particular attention to one heavy-duty cord. Dan couldn't unplug it, so draped it from workbench to workbench making sure it would be several feet off the floor. He pulled the power cord for the band saw from the wall and coiled it around the table. He was walking over to the breaker panel to shut off the power to the lathe and mill when he heard someone come in. Dan assumed it was Ed coming to help. He turned to tell him to go fire up his dozer so they could divert the water.

Suddenly, he heard Syd's high-pitched barking over the downpour. When he looked, he saw a tall man standing in the doorway. Dan did not notice the gun at first because the intruder was partly in shadow. Instead, he was struck by the unusual posture of the figure, holding both arms out in front of him. It was then he noticed the pistol in the man's hands.

It was Paulo Kraus.

"Stop where you are," Paulo commanded.

Dan could not place the accent. It sounded somewhat Hispanic but was different. He stopped and raised his hands to shoulder height.

"Where are the files the old man stole?" Paulo looked around the shop. Several tables were being used for cutting and assembling metal pieces. Most of the tables were made of metal, but a few were made of wood. He scanned the room while keeping an eye on Dan. There was a heavy, metal worktable between the two men, and neither could see below the waist of their opponent. To Paulo's right were steel cabinets and he could see some sandpaper and paint supplies inside the open door of one of them. The binder and files could be hidden in there. Farther back in the shop he saw partially assembled products, but nothing else.

"Look, pal, I need to shut those breakers off or we're both going to be electrocuted," Dan said, motioning his head toward the subpanels.

"You move very slowly and don't try anything." Paulo could feel the water, already at ankle-deep and it was rising fast.

Dan inched over toward the panel and pushed the first few breakers.

"Leave the lights on," Paulo commanded, knowing he would lose the advantage in an unfamiliar shop in the dark.

"There's a light just outside and an emergency light at the other end there. The other lights are plugged into outlets near the floor."

"No!" Paulo gestured emphatically with the gun.

"I promise I won't do anything. Let me turn it off, and I won't move until our eyes adjust. But we have about another two inches before we fry."

With that, Dan hit the last breaker causing the majority of the lights to go off. As he predicted, the light outside the open door flooded the room. A small battery-powered emergency light at the other end came on and provided enough light to make out most objects in the area. Dan waited to hear a blast from the intruder's gun.

After a few seconds when no shot came, Dan spoke again. "We good?" He could see the backlit figure had not moved and still had the gun on him. "What's so important about those files?"

"They were stolen at the end of the war and do not belong to you or your country." The anonymity of the dark made Paulo comfortable sharing information. "My grandfather worked on those projects and my family has more right to them than anyone." Paulo was not going to volunteer any information about the hunt for gold, though.

"What are you planning? Building V-1 bombs? Maybe an atomic bomb? Are you going to try to make a time machine and bring Hitler back to rule the world?"

"You know more than I thought about the work, but no, we don't plan any of that. Time travel? Ha!

"Why would you want seventy-year-old information on experiments? The technology is outdated."

"Because it was my grandfather's lifelong dream to bring the collective work to light. If the world knew what the Germans were doing, it would be clear that we should have won the war. If we had not been led by crazy men who got so distracted by the Jewish issue, we would have crushed you under our boots."

"You call the murder of six million people an issue?" Dan interrupted. He couldn't believe the arrogance.

"Even in the area of physics," Paulo continued, ignoring the question, "the old-school German physicists held us back because they thought there were too many Jews associated with relativity theory and quantum physics. They called my grandfather 'white Jew' and formed their own brand of physics, Deutsche Physik that set us back years. At the end of the war, he was exiled and his work stolen by the Americans and Russians."

"This is all about proving your grandfather was right?" Dan was incredulous. "You come up here and kill a man to show that your grandfather was right seventy years ago?"

"It wasn't only the technology the US stole. They stole all of our files and records. I need those records." Paulo glared at the clueless American.

"You think Willis had your precious records?"

"I know he did. The old man, Willis, his greed led me to him. Greed for gold and treasure that rightfully belongs to the Reich and my family." Paulo's temper had gotten the best of him and the part about the gold slipped out. It didn't matter now. He'd lock this one up with the other one below the garage and be long gone before they would be found.

"You think he had a stash of Nazi gold?" Dan scoffed. "He was living on a pension and drove a fifteen-year-old car."

"Willis started researching the records for German shipments of uranium to Japan during his work in the 1950s. As a member of the Axis powers, we were working with them in the race to build a nuclear bomb. Subs were used to transport the uranium to Japan. Then he discovered that Tokyo paid for the uranium in gold, shipped back on the same subs. Some of the subs were redirected to South America when it became apparent we would lose, and a few of them sank. When he retired, he decided to look for the subs that went missing near Argentina. That was how we learned of his hunt for the gold. He came to my country a few years ago and hired a ship to search. Our network was notified immediately when a foreigner began scouring the waters off our coast. He had no luck, so came back here to do more research." Paulo waved his arm around to indicate this is where Willis returned.

"So you tracked him back here?"

Paulo laughed. "No. We lost him, but your Agent Stevens helped with that. We got Stevens interested by sending bogus emails and inquiries so he would lead us to the scientist. I followed Stevens to Willis. Once I knew where Willis was, the next day I made sure I got to him before Stevens. I was just going to look around, but Willis caught me. He came at me. That old man picked up a hammer." He shook his head, remembering. "I blocked it and backhanded him, but when he fell his head hit the metal of the car lift."

"So you lowered it onto his head and crushed it?"

"No. I was lowering it to look inside the car, in case it had anything of value in it. He was lying beside the lift. I was on the other side where the controls are. At the last second, he moved and ended up under it. His scream was so loud I panicked and ran away. His wife must be deaf not to have heard it."

"But you stuck around the area."

"There was nothing to tie me to his death, and I was pretty sure he had some copies of our documents based on things he had revealed during the search on the ship. My grandfather kept an eye on him from Argentina as best he could."

"So you were watching Willis, and Stevens was tracking you?"

The big man was growing weary of the questions. "Wrong again. Stevens is a moron. We planted someone in his department. It took years for her to get close. She makes all their travel arrangements. If we wanted to find someone, all we had to do is create a few web searches on certain topics and then watch Stevens. As he did with Willis, he would soon lead us to them trying to protect his precious secrets. We used to have to do it more clandestinely. The Internet has made it so much easier. We could spin him up with a few web searches, or a call or two on a phone we knew was compromised. We won't need her now if we have the documents."

Dan looked down. The water in the shop was over his ankles and still rising. He took a half a step to his left. With the light now behind Paulo, he could see the water level was consistent across the shop floor and that Paulo's feet were also in the water.

Syd's barking was so high pitched and frantic that Dan could occasionally hear it over the rain.

"What's in those cabinets?" Paulo demanded as he gestured with the gun toward the metal cabinets.

"Mostly shop stuff." Dan raised his arm and pointed to the first one with the door open. "That one has mostly painting supplies. The one next to it has materials for doing fiberglass molds. Those have power tools and extension cords."

When he saw Paulo redirect his attention to the cabinets, Dan took a few quick steps to his right. The large welding table between him and Paulo had a thick steel top and blocked the gunman's view of Dan from the waist down.

"What do you do here? I grew up on my grandfather's ranch and

203

we didn't have a shop like this."

"I didn't grow up here. I grew up in town. My father and uncle were always tinkering with cars and machines. I still help on the ranch but talked them into letting me build a machine shop. I do a little work on the side." Dan smiled and pointed to a large milling machine on the other end of the room. "You see that machine there? It's used, came from the Lawrence Livermore Lab. It may have done some work on one of your grandfather's projects."

Dan knew this would get Paulo's attention. When Paulo turned his head, Dan lifted his right foot and stepped into the cut-off barrel of kerosene his uncle had used to clean the chain the other day. It made a plopping sound, but the rain on the roof drowned it out.

"Where are the files?" Paulo was growing impatient.

"I don't have them."

"Why should I believe you?"

Paulo waded carefully toward the cabinets, looking down and moving his feet slowly. It would be the most logical place to store them. He grabbed the handle of the first one and pulled. Water poured into the bottom. When Paulo looked down, Dan lifted his left foot and stepped completely into the barrel of kerosene. Paulo set his backpack down on the closest workbench and dug out a small flashlight. He pointed it inside the cabinet but saw nothing except engine parts. He moved to the next one.

"The files are not in any of those, and all you're doing is getting my stuff wet." Dan tried not to show his annoyance. He looked down. The water was still rising and was now only about four inches from the top of the plastic barrel in which he now stood. Soon it would flow over the side and mix with the kerosene.

Paulo ignored him and moved to the second cabinet, repeating the process of opening and searching through it. Again, water poured into the bottom covering whatever was stored there. He continued to the third of the five cabinets.

"Why did you shoot Agent Stevens if you are such a nonviolent man?" Dan picked up some thick rubber gloves on the worktable in front of him and put them on. They were black and would be hard to see in the dim light, especially with Paulo ruining his night vision with the flashlight.

"He saw me beside the road and I was sure he recognized me." Paulo talked without turning around. "I couldn't let him apprehend me. Besides, I didn't shoot to kill."

"Shooting through a windshield at night, you came within about six inches of his heart. I think you give yourself too much credit."

"You Americans are so arrogant. If I really wanted to kill him, I could have easily gone down into the ravine and shot him again. How do you say it? Finished him off?" He glanced over his shoulder to make sure Dan didn't move. "All I wanted to do was disable him so I could get away."

"You shot a man in the shoulder, he crashed into some boulders, and you left him alone in the middle of nowhere to die. I would say you did more than disable him." Dan couldn't help getting angry. This guy caused him a lot of grief. "You've killed one man already. You damn near killed my uncle. You shot a federal agent, and now you're waving my gun around at me."

"I'm sorry, I forgot my manners. I meant to thank you for the weapon." Paulo smiled at the irony. "As soon as you give me the files, I'll be on my way."

The mention of Wally seemed to surprise Paulo. Dan decided to press the verbal attack. "They know who you are. The police have a description of the vehicle you're driving. They're probably closing down the roads and watching all the airports. How do you propose to get out of the country even if you find your precious files?" Dan wanted to keep the guy talking.

"Maybe I'll take you with me. You probably know these hills pretty well. You could be my personal guide." If he could make it the three hundred or so miles south and cross into Mexico, he would be able to fly home. Crossing the border into Mexico was easy. Escaping the hills could be tricky. With only three roads out, it was easy for the police to block the routes.

Dan slowly picked up the heavy-duty cord he had draped from table-to-table. He took a rag off the top of the bench and began wiping it off as best he could. Trying to conceal it, Dan slowly took off his right glove and lowered the thick wire to waist level. With his ungloved hand, he began picking at some electrical tape wrapped around the thick cord.

Paulo was standing at the fourth cabinet. He had a bit of trouble opening this one because the mechanism was bent. The water was also high enough to make it harder to open the doors. It required Paulo to open them a bit, let the water run in to equalize the pressure, then swing the doors the rest of the way. He still had no luck finding the binder or files.

Dan had the tape that was around the outside of the bundle of wires removed. The three wires inside were also individually wrapped with tape. He held the thick cord with the gloved hand and spread the wrapped wires away from each other, then began removing the tape on the first one.

Since the last cabinet door was ajar, Paulo swung it open further and shined the light inside. There were more paint cans, mostly spray paint and some primer. Still no files. With the cabinets searched, he turned around to face Dan. As he did, Syd appeared in the doorway. She was crouched down, ears back, and emitting a low growl.

Worried she would get hurt, Dan immediately commanded, "Syd, no!" She stopped in place but did not take her eyes off the intruder. "Syd, up. Sit." She glanced at Dan, then jumped on the wooden table just inside the door and moved to a sitting position, facing Paulo. "Stay, dammit." She sat there shaking with coiled energy wanting to attack. Dan realized she must have clawed her way out of the sliding windows in the rear of the cab.

The two men turned their attention to each other.

"What are you doing?" Paulo could not see well at first, so he shined the flashlight on Dan. Dan's hands were below the level of the workbench so Paulo could not see what he was doing, but obviously he was working at something. "Let me see your hands."

Dan raised the ungloved hand up to about chest level. "Just trying to fix this cord," he lied. "I meant to get to it earlier." He busied himself exposing the second of the three wires. With two of the three done, he was able to give it a good tug and the third one separated, exposing the extension cord's wires.

Paulo did not like this new development but was not sure what Dan was planning. "Put it down, or I'll shoot you."

"Oh, you don't want me to do that. You see, this here is a two-hundred-and-twenty-volt, three-phase line that comes directly in from outside. It's not up to code because it doesn't run through a breaker box. Do you know anything about electricity?" He looked at Paulo as if they were having a casual conversation.

"A little."

"Well, usually if something shorted out by falling into water, the breaker would trip and you'd just get a bad jolt." He held up the cord. "But since this one isn't on a breaker, the energy would keep flowing until you caught on fire." He paused to let the image sink in. "See, this ranch has been here a hundred years, and sometimes things got overlooked when it came to building codes and safety. I've been after my uncle to get this corrected, but he hasn't gotten to it yet."

Paulo began to look around for something to jump on, but all of the worktables near him were made of steel and would conduct electricity. Then it struck him. "If you do that you will die, too."

"You're gonna kill me anyway, so…" Dan waved the wire around. He made sure it was in the gloved hand.

"You're not that crazy. I could shoot you." Paulo was too far into

207

the shop to leap for the door.

"If you shoot me, I'll drop it for sure." He let his ungloved hand drop below the table so Paulo couldn't see it.

"Keep your hands where I can see them." Paulo raised the gun level with Dan's face.

Dan brought his right hand up and let the tape he had removed drop into the water with a loud plop. This elicited a little scream from Paulo.

Dan said in a calm voice, "You scared me, now see what you've done."

Paulo was breathing hard. He almost hyperventilated when he saw the tape drop. "You crazy son of a bitch. I should kill you."

"Go ahead and shoot. "Don't worry." Dan waved the gloved hand "This is the live wire."

Paulo decided to negotiate his way out. "Just give me the files, and I'll let you live."

"No. I think you should drop the gun." Dan smiled. "If you do, I'll let you live." Thankfully, in the dark Paulo could not see how badly Dan's hands were shaking.

Paulo moved toward the door, making Syd growl. He stopped.

"Too late, bucko. You either drop the gun, or I'm gonna light this place up. I got nothin' to lose." Dan slid his gloved hand so it was about three feet away from the exposed portion of the wire.

Paulo raised the gun again. "Drop the wire on the table. You're standing in the same water so you'll die with me." When Paulo extended the gun toward Dan's face, Syd snarled and rose into a position to jump. "And so will your annoying dog," Paulo said, swinging the gun in Syd's direction.

With the threat to Syd, Dan was now more angry than scared. He glanced down at his feet to ensure the water was not overflowing into the barrel, then looked at Paulo and smiled. "No!"

With that, Dan let the exposed portion of the power cord hit the water. There were sparks, and a blue crackle of energy seemed to cover the entire floor of the shop. He could hear popping sounds, and Paulo's screams as the voltage hit his body. The gun flew out of Paulo's hand and he fell against a metal table in spasms, sliding to the floor. It was all Dan could do to keep his balance and not touch anything around him.

Finally, he yanked the cord out of the water. It was sizzling and sparked as the heat from the electricity evaporated any water that existed between the wires. Dan stood shaking for a few seconds as he watched the blue glow dissipate from the water's surface. It was several minutes before he felt safe enough to step out of the kerosene and into the water.

Paulo lay dead on the floor, his hair still smoking. Dan was stunned because he had only expected it to knock the gunman down. Trembling, he walked over to a metal drum he used as a trash can, braced his hands on both sides and threw up into the barrel. The smell of the electrocuted body, along with the adrenaline coursing through him, almost made Dan pass out.

Syd moved to the end of the table where she could reach Dan and licked his face as he leaned over recovering. "Good girl, Syd," Dan said between deep breaths when he could finally stop heaving.

It took several more minutes before he could make it to the door and fresh air.

Michael L. Patton

CHAPTER 20 - THURSDAY MAY 20TH

Wally had a follow-up visit scheduled at the head-trauma center in Santa Clara. Since Dan and Ed needed to go into town to pick up a few power tools to replace those they lost in the incident, they all rode together in Ed's truck.

Dan had also promised the detectives he would stop by to sign the statement they took from him after his encounter with Paulo. They had copied the file from his cell phone, which had been recording, and had it transcribed by a stenographer. An FBI agent had accompanied the sheriff and CHP personnel when Dan called the authorities, and he had gladly handed over the files and binders to be forwarded to Stevens.

Wally's doctor walked up to them in the waiting room with a big smile. "Mr. Williams, your tests all came back normal." He patted Wally on the shoulder.

Wally's head dropped as he let out a heavy sigh. "Doc, something must be wrong."

"Why? What do you mean?" The doctor looked confused and concerned he'd missed something.

"Cause I ain't never been normal in my whole life." Wally broke into a smile. Dan and Ed laughed.

"Get out of here," the doctor said in mock anger. "And I don't ever want to see you again."

"Thanks, Doc."

The three of them exited the hospital joking and picking on Wally.

At the sheriff's headquarters, Dan was told that neither Sanchez nor Thronson was in. One of the other detectives took Dan into the office and found the forms he needed to sign. Even though he only came in to sign the papers, it made him nervous to be in the building where he had been held. He took care of the paperwork and hurried

the other two out of there. As they were exiting the building, they
saw Spinelli pull up across the street.

"Hey, Spinelli, I hear the motor pool put a bed in the trunk of
your cruiser," Dan yelled as Spinelli jogged across to meet them.

"How are you, my friend? What are you being charged with
now?" He winked at Dan.

"I'm getting the heck out of Dodge, man. Hey, we were gonna
grab some lunch. Care to join us?"

"Sure. There's a pretty good sandwich shop around the corner."
Spinelli pointed to his right.

"Lead the way."

They walked to the end of the block and another block down. The
group entered a small deli with tables in the rear. Dan could tell by
the smells that hit him when he walked in the food would be great.
The lunch crowd was just starting, so they stood in line and put in
their orders. At the cashier, Dan announced, "It's on me."

Dan paid for the food then they walked to a corner table. Sanchez
and Thronson were sitting at the next table. They stood up to shake
hands all around.

"No hard feelings?" Thronson asked as he shook Dan's hand.

"No hard feelings," Dan said and smiled.

"Heck, he even bought me lunch," said Spinelli, holding up his
sandwich.

"Oh, trying to bribe an officer, huh?" Thronson joked.

Dan laughed. "If it weren't for these three, I'd be on trial for
murder. A sandwich is cheap."

Ed gave him a funny look.

Dan smiled at him. "I had a chat with Captain O'Shea about your
horse-trading skills."

Ed winked at him.

"Don't forget Syd the Wonderdog," Spinelli chimed in.

"Of course, where would we all be without Syd?" Wally said

without a trace of sarcasm. "Smartest dog in the world."

"Dan, I meant to ask you," Sanchez said. "How the heck did you have the balls to drop that cord in the water? Weren't you afraid it would get you too?"

"Not at all. You see, I have this wise uncle, who used to drive a truck hauling gas, and he told me petroleum products like gas or kerosene don't conduct electricity. That barrel was made of plastic, and I had rubber-soled shoes on, so I figured I was triple insulated." Dan laughed, slapped Wally on the back and bit into his sandwich. A silence fell over the group.

Finally, Spinelli spoke up. "You know why, don't you?"

Everyone stared at him, so he continued. "You see, petroleum molecules form covalent bonds and water molecules form ionic bonds."

More blank stares.

"In a covalent bond, the atoms actually share an electron. So both atoms think they have a complete set and form a very stable bond between them. In ionic bonds, one atom steals an electron from the other, creating a negative charge on the atom from which it was taken. So it goes looking for an electron to regain its balance. That's why it conducts electricity so well."

He could see they were not sure whether to believe him.

"I majored in law enforcement but minored in chemistry in college. Thought about doing the whole CSI thing. You know, working in the lab."

"Well thank you, Mr. Science." Dan finally let him off the hook. "I don't know about the whole covert bonding thing." He purposely butchered the word covalent. "The only Bond I know is 007. But I do know I can believe my uncle when he tells me something."

"You just keep on believing that, big guy," Wally told Dan, and winked at the rest of them.

THE END

Dear Reader,

Thank you for reading this book. If you have borrowed this book through Amazon's Kindle Unlimited e-Book subscription program, I kindly ask that you close the book here or at the end. This will ensure that the author is properly credited for the book borrow. Thank you. If you enjoyed Death in the Devil's Range, would you please write an honest review? You have no idea how much it means to get a new review. You will also help all the people out there who use reviews to make decisions. Thank you so much.

If you enjoyed Dan, Wally and Syd and their special relationship, sign up for my guaranteed SPAM-free mailing list.

https://mailchi.mp/870edbe6ec1c/michaelpattonwritessignup

You can follow more frequent information and news about the author at his blog here:

https://michaelpatton.blog

Or if you would like to send me a note directly use the following email address.

michael.patton.writes@gmail.com

Let me know what you think, and I'll also let you know when my next book is available.

ABOUT THE AUTHOR

Michael has been writing poetry and short stories since he was in the third grade. He has had several articles published about his motorcycle adventures and been included in a regional anthology of poetry and stories. After thirty years in the telecommunications industry, he decided to retire and now has time to focus more on his writing. This is his first foray into novels, so please leave a review to let him know what you think. He lives in northern California with his wife and his best friend Cyrus, their cat.

If you enjoyed this book…

Read Dan, Wally, and Syd's next adventure!

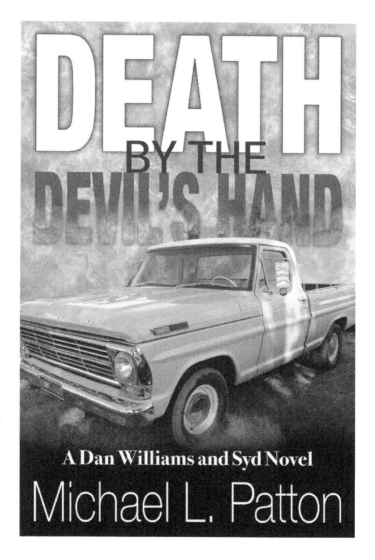

Buy it on Amazon

Made in the USA
Middletown, DE
11 March 2020